The Butterfly's Dance

Christyna Hunter

Wasteland Press
Shelbyville, KY USA
www.wastelandpress.net

The Butterfly's Dance
by Christyna Hunter

Second Printing – September 2007
ISBN: 1-933265-73-6

Printed in the U.S.A.

To Vicky, who helped me become my own butterfly

What the caterpillar calls the end of the world, the master calls a butterfly.

-Richard Bach

Illusions: The Adventures of a Reluctant Messiah

(Delacorte Press)

Acknowledgements

I would like to thank the following people who assisted me in the creation and development of this, my very first novel.

Dr. Robin Merlino, who answered my medical questions about spinal cord injury; Y. Marie Arrington, who, in passing many years ago said that maybe I should write a book one day; Sarah Banks, who learned she could indeed sit down for eight hours straight and read a book to edit it; my parents, who never once told me I couldn't do or be anything I wanted to be.

Prologue

Duncan, Virginia

Bone chilling wind whipped through Kayla and tossed her shoulder length hair into disarray. Shifting her stuffed backpack higher up her shoulder, she clenched her chattering teeth and hugged her arms about her numbed body. Puffs of air formed and dissolved as she breathed. Vigorously, she rubbed her hands together to create warmth.

The frigid January temperature didn't put a damper on her mounting temper, however.

Geez, mom, hurry up!

Tapping her foot, Kayla mentally berated old Mrs. Zimmer, who'd insisted Kayla stay after school for help with her math. True, she was barely pulling a C, but who needed math anyway? Why bother learning decimals and fractions when there were calculators? Her mom pulled one out every time she balanced her checkbook. And every time, her mother cursed because there was never enough money. If having money, or more likely, *not* having money, meant this much heartache, why worsen it by learning math? Just use a calculator and be done with it.

I'm freezing!

Now, instead of spending valuable time on more important things, she was standing outside Duncan Elementary School, freezing her tush off, waiting for her lackadaisical mother to show up.

"Hey, Kay, where's your mom?"

Oh, geez, not Tommy!

Her day just went from bad to worse.

Kayla rolled her eyes as Tommy Madison, class nerd, approached. Although they were the same age, Tommy was six inches shorter, with thick-rimmed eyeglasses perched upon his sloped nose. His white cotton shirt was tucked tightly into a pair of brown corduroys that rode several inches above his hip. With his own bulging backpack, he trudged towards Kayla.

Glancing around, she made sure no one witnessed her unwanted interaction with Tommy. If word got out that she'd said one word to him, her social life would be ruined. This unexpected meeting with the class nerd would mar her reputation as *the* coolest girl in the sixth grade. God, could her life get any worse?

Oh, Mooommm!

"My mom's late. Scram," Kayla muttered through her chattering teeth.

"Can't. Gotta wait for my mom, too."

Disappointed that Tommy hadn't gotten the hint, Kayla was about to argue with him again when she caught sight of her mama's car out of the corner of her eye. Her body warmed slightly at the thought of the shelter the car would provide. With an impatient eagerness to get out of the cold and away from Tommy, she watched the brown Nova pull up to the curb. Upon close inspection, she eyed the chipped brown paint and missing right front hubcap with annoyance. Geez, would her parents ever have enough money to get a *real* car?

"See ya tomorrow, Kay."

Cringing, she opened the car door and slid inside.

"Hey, baby, how was school today?" Mama asked cheerfully.

"Fine." Her mother always wanted a lengthy explanation of her day, but Kayla never felt like describing it in more than one word.

As they left the school's parking lot and got on the main highway, her mother spoke. "It's taken us awhile to settle into this new town, honey. I know you've been begging to start up your dancing lessons again."

Kayla's heart stopped.

"Well, I made it over to the town rec center and signed you up for ballet classes," Mama continued. "You'll go every Saturday morning beginning in two weeks."

"Yipeeeee!" Kayla shouted. Finally! Dance classes.

Excitement spread like wildfire from her heart to tickle her toes and fingers.

She loved to dance. No, not loved, but lived, breathed, dancing. She knew she was going to be a famous ballerina someday.

Tap dancing had been a little too fast. The soles of her feet blistered, her knees ached as they tried to keep up with the rhythm. The music was fun to listen to, but it just hurt too much to keep up with the beat. And that non-stop *clang* of the shoes clapping against the floor made her head pound.

Ballet was different. Better. The music was quiet, simple. You could keep up with it. The pirouette and the plie` were so grand, like princesses would do. The costumes were fun, too. The pink leotards and tutus allowed her to not only wear her favorite color, but to look like royalty, too. And instead of the clanging of tap shoes, there was only a quiet *swish* of the slippers.

When she was four, she saw a musical on television that had Leslie Caron dancing through the streets of Paris with Gene Kelly. And Kayla was instantly hooked. She practiced whenever she had the chance. She played records in the living room and danced until her legs and body throbbed. And then she danced some more.

For brief moments, she forgot that her parents couldn't afford to buy her a new outfit or the latest Barbie. While the music played, she was lost in *her* world, made of kings and queens, good and evil, weak and strong. She would begin weak, but through the dance, she became strong. In the end, all the people in her imaginary world loved her and made her the queen of all the lands.

Unlike her Aunt Eve.

Kayla had proudly announced to her aunt her plans to be a dancer. Once. Her aunt's response had been, "That's cute dear, but why not be a teacher?" Her grandmother didn't even smile when Kayla told her. She'd frowned and shook her head, like she did when Kayla had broken a dish. Well, screw her! She'd heard her father say *screw* when he was mad at somebody. She thought it appropriate for her Aunt Eve and grandma now. She was a big girl now, practically a woman, and could make up her own mind. She was going to be a dancer.

She'd begged her parents for forever and ever to go back to ballet class. After months and months, it seemed her bugging had finally paid off.

Kayla took brief notice that her mother had stopped at a red light. Her coat was unbuttoned now, the car's heater slowly defrosting her frigid body. She only half listened as her mother jabbered on about the different errands she'd run that day. As she rambled, Kayla looked through the car's window. Snow mounds at least six feet tall rested on each of the intersection's four corners. The first real snow storm of the winter had dumped several feet of snow over the weekend. Kayla and her classmates were overjoyed that school was closed the day before, but grumbled when they had to return today.

The light turned green, allowing the car in front of the Nova to ease out into the intersection. Listening to her mama drone on about her day, Kayla's ears suddenly took in the sound of screeching tires. The sound grew increasingly closer. Closer. *Closer.*

As she turned her head to the right, a big dump truck traveling at what Kayla thought was the speed of light hurdled towards her. The high pitch shrill of the truck's tires grew louder, and she coved her ears. But the sound continued to get louder. Louder. *Louder.*

Part of her screamed while the other part was too dazed to yell. In shocked horror, she simply watched in slow motion as the truck's front end rammed into her side of the decrepit Nova. Metal scraped metal, bending the Nova as if it were a twig. Kayla was shoved to the left, then right. Mangled metal tore the flesh of her right arm and leg. She was too shaken to cry out the scream of pain that was lodged in her throat. She suddenly was pitched forward. Pain reluctantly registered in her brain. Blood soaked her leg. The car stopped moving. But the sudden pause in motion didn't stop Kayla from continuing forward. Unable to fight gravity, her head slammed into the dashboard.

The screeching tires and the pulsating pain faded into blessed darkness.

Chapter One

Duncan, Virginia
Eighteen Years Later

She was dancing.

A field of white lilies gliding on a sea of green grass surrounded her. The cool breeze carried with it the scent of lilies warmed by the sun. The sky was a cloudless, endless, shimmering blue.

And she was dancing.

She wore a white blouse and matching skirt that reflected the sun's toasty rays. As she twirled in delicate circles, her skirt lifted, caught by the flowing breeze. The rush of air cooled her skin, making her feel light, weightless. She felt so free, as if the breeze carried her. Her feet never touched the ground, but rather slid through the air, agile and smooth. She spun in endless, intoxicating circles. She felt so free, so free...

"Good morning everyone. It's now 6:30 A.M. on a lovely May morning, and time now for the latest news."

Abruptly, cruelly, the dream ended. Thanks to the radio alarm, Kayla was yanked back to reality. Too soon. As if the efficient, business-like talk of the deejay wasn't jarring enough, she woke up thinking she was free.

But she wasn't.

Groggy, she pulled herself up to a sitting position as she struggled to find her bearings. It had all felt so real. Her legs tingled still. But when she tried to move them, they wouldn't budge. As the dream faded, bright hope dissolved into slick disappointment. Reality sucked.

Kayla sighed, shut off the alarm clock, yawned, and shuffled herself to the side of the bed. Pulling herself into the wheelchair, she spewed a few obscenities along the way. Once she was in the chair, she wheeled herself to the bathroom.

As she showered, she couldn't get the dream completely out of her mind. It flickered in her mind, images fading and brightening like old movies from the 1920's. It felt so real, and brought back a long forgotten memory of dancing in her parents' living room, giggling as she spun to the beats that purred through the stereo's speakers. Snatching the memory back as it begun to unfold, Kayla chided herself for being a daydreamer.

When she got out of the shower, she wiped off the steamed mirror and stared at her reflection. Since her long, midnight black hair was wet, it didn't have the slight curl at its tips that it did when it was dry. Her light green eyes, prominent on her slightly peach colored face, were now awake and bright. Adorning a light green pant suit and matching shoes, she checked her reflection once more. Satisfied with the mild application of soft, rosy blush and even softer color of lip gloss, she left the bathroom. When she entered the kitchen, Sammy greeted her.

"Good morning, Mr. Sam. And how are you?"

Sammy meowed his response as he jumped into her lap. She scratched his chin and he purred in delighted pleasure. He stayed in her lap until she reached the counter, then jumped up onto it to patiently wait for his breakfast. She poured him his food and wheeled to the refrigerator for a glass of orange juice and a bagel.

By eight fifteen, Kayla sat behind her desk at her downtown office, reading a file on a new client. She'd received James Michaels's folder a week ago from his high school counselor. This new client looked interesting. As a vocational counselor for the disabled, Kayla had read many files similar to Mr. Michaels's. However, this one, for some reason she couldn't put her finger on, was different.

Reading, she discovered James was eighteen and had multiple sclerosis. His MS had been diagnosed when he was fifteen, which was very unusual. Her professional experience told her that most individuals were diagnosed with MS in their twenties or thirties. James's parents had died a year ago in a car crash and he'd been in his uncle's care since then. He'd just graduated from high school with a GPA of three point five, a note of great accomplishment, in her opinion, considering his circumstances. Recently, his MS had flared up, making him weak and causing him to use a wheelchair.

Kayla knew it would be difficult to place this young man in a job. The unpredictability of MS often made it hard for those with the disease to find stable employment. However, he was coming in for assistance and encouragement, and she would do the best she could.

Thinking of this young man's predicament made her mind wander again. Crystal clear memories flooded her heart. Where once she could move freely, gracefully, without a thought or care, she was now frozen into partial immobility.

The sickening, belittling feeling of having others move her body had consumed Kayla once she'd woken up in the hospital after the accident. Even more maddening was the fact that there was not a damn thing she could do about it. She'd lie in her hospital bed, refusing to speak, to listen. But once her mother had healed from the accident, she and her father pushed Kayla into rehabilitation. Her mother, usually easygoing and cheery, harassed her daughter relentlessly.

Weary, her body broken, her soul empty, she'd slowly recuperated. Hours of sweaty physical therapy became her whole existence. During the whole period of her physical rehabilitation, no one asked her how she felt emotionally, how she felt having lost the use of half her body. No one wanted to look on the inside and see what emotional scars the car accident had left behind. No one seemed to care, so she tried not to care either.

The phone rang and Kayla's thoughts quickly scattered. "Good morning, this is Kayla Jennings. How may I help you?"

"Hey, sis, I was calling to check on our plans for tonight."

Pleasure replaced the sorrow of remembering the past. Hearing Maggie's voice could do that. Maggie had saved Kayla's life in so many ways. She smiled at Maggie calling her "sis." They were not biological sisters. They had met in college and had become each other's support systems. Both she and Maggie were only children, left to raise their parents on their own. It was a joke they shared often. They had that and a passion for movies that bonded them since meeting so many years ago. A sister of the heart was so much more precious than a blood sister. A sister of the heart was carefully selected. Kayla had always been pleased with her choice.

"Hey there, Maggie. I think I can still pencil you in. Seven o'clock, right?"

"Very funny! 'Pencil you in.' Yeah, I'll meet you at the theater at seven. Don't be late."

Kayla huffed. "I'm never late. I'll see you then."

She hung up the phone and continued reading the file on James Michaels. All thoughts of her past and this morning's dream had dissipated. At least, for the time being.

An hour later, the receptionist buzzed her office. "Kayla, Mr. Michaels is here."

"Thank you, Jenny. Please send him back."

A moment later, there was a soft tap at the door. "Please come in," Kayla replied.

The door opened, and a young man with black, wavy hair that barely touched the collar of his khaki shirt, wheeled himself into her office. Kayla also took notice of bags under his sea green eyes. As she began to greet James Michaels, another man walked in and shut the door. As he turned, she took in a quick breath of admiration. Okay, lust. She would admit, only to herself, it was lust that caused her breathing to halt and her mouth to water.

He was tall, at least six feet. His hair was the softest shade of blonde, like hay that had been out in the sun for awhile. A dark blue sweater and jeans molded his trim body. Too comfortably, she thought. She caught herself staring, swallowed hard, and redirected her attention to the younger man.

"Hello, Mr. Michaels."

"Hello, Ms. Jennings. Please call me Jim. This is Jordan Michaels, my uncle."

Although her voice threatened to quiver due to her thudding heart and rushing hormones, she calmly said, "Hello, Jim, Mr. Michaels."

In a calm voice and with a soft smile, Jordan Michaels responded, "No need for formalities. Please, call me Jordan."

"Well, Jim, Jordan, let's begin. What can I do for you, Jim?"

"I've just graduated from high school."

"Yes, I saw that you graduated with a three point five GPA. Congratulations. I'm sure you worked hard to achieve that."

Jim blushed slightly. "Yeah, well, I had hoped to be a pilot, but...you know, stuff happened."

His smile reminded Kayla of a similar smile she'd worn many years ago, a smile to lighten the mood and deflect others from seeing the pain deep within.

"Since things aren't going as I'd planned," Jim continued, "I need help figuring out what to do now."

Jim talked about how his MS had recently weakened him to the point of requiring a wheelchair. He also mentioned the help his uncle had given him in the last year since the death of his parents. Kayla was tempted to look at Jordan and see his reaction. She also wanted to look into those soft aquamarine eyes of his again.

"Well, Jim, we can start slowly. We can have you participate in a vocational assessment evaluation. This evaluation helps us discover your vocational strengths and weaknesses. I see here that you got straight A's in all of your English classes. Do you enjoy writing?"

"A little."

"A little? He wrote creative writing essays on everything from flying to dancing. He's a terrific writer."

It was the first time Kayla had heard from Jordan since he had told her his name. After resisting for several moments, her gaze traveled from Jim to Jordan. Jordan was smiling, a gleam of pride in his eyes. She acknowledged his deep love for Jim, and felt a pang of envy.

"Ah, Uncle Jordan, come on." He blushed. "Yes, I like to write. And I do an okay job at it."

"Okay? *Okay?* Jim, you got an 'A' every semester—"

"Uncle Jordan!" Jim cut him off with a warning, even though a grin was tugging his lips upward.

"If you enjoy writing *and* are good at it, it would be a place to start," Kayla explained. "If you want, we can still do the vocational evaluation, to give us a broader base to work with."

Jim and Kayla continued their interview for the next half-hour, discussing Jim's strengths and weaknesses, likes and dislikes. Finally, Kayla announced, "It looks as if everything is taken care of. You can come in next Wednesday morning at nine for the first round of the evaluation. Mark, our certified vocational evaluator, will conduct the evaluation. Now, let me see you two out."

As she drew her wheelchair back from the desk, she hesitated. She wanted to impress Jordan, even though, at the same time, she thought it was ridiculous. She and men never mixed. It just didn't happen. Hadn't experience taught her that already? Well, hell, there was no point in dwelling on it. She'd done that in the past. But not anymore. It was silly that she even thought, for a microsecond, that it mattered.

After what she hoped was only a brief hesitation, she continued pulling back on the chair then stopped by the door, waiting for Jim and Jordan to go ahead. Jordan got up and held the door for Jim. Jordan held the door for her as well. Surprised, she could only mumble a thank you as she wheeled by. He just smiled and nodded.

Once the three of them reached the lobby, Kayla wished Jim good luck on the vocational evaluation. As Jordan began to leave, Jim excused himself to use the restroom.

"I can come along if you want help, Jim," Jordan whispered, but Kayla was still able to hear.

"I'm old enough, thank you. Stop babying me, especially in public," Jim tersely whispered to his uncle, his eyelids narrowed.

Jordan held the door for his nephew. Once Jim had left, Jordan turned around, rolled his eyes, and smiled that beautifully male smile. "Kids!" he said sarcastically.

She couldn't help but laugh. His smile was contagious. "I'll see Jim next week. Have a good week, Mr. Mich—Jordan."

"Goodbye."

She returned to her office and shut the door. As she tried to concentrate on the file of the next client, Jordan Michaels kept permeating her thoughts. It made her uncomfortable. Her experiences with men were short, painful. But as she listed every reason why she should forget about him, her mind kept pulling up Jordan's face, with his irresistible smile and his vivid blue eyes.

Chapter Two

"You sure you feel up to staying at the nursery for awhile?" asked Jordan.

"You bet," answered Jim.

"Cause if you don't, I can take the afternoon off."

"No. It's cool." Jim glanced over at his uncle who was driving the van. Jordan didn't look convinced.

"I feel good today. Really." Tired, but that was nothing new. He'd been continually tired for the last six months. The leg tremors mostly came at night, which disturbed his sleep. And Uncle Jordan's.

In the last year since Jim's parents' death, and especially the few months when the MS had flared up more, Jim's uncle had some sort of radar that sensed when Jim was suffering. There wasn't too much to be done. Sometimes the medication worked. Sometimes it didn't. Jim was always grateful that his uncle was there for the rough times, but he also felt guilty. His uncle's life now only revolved around his nephew and the nursery. That left little time for fun.

"Sure?"

Jim rolled his eyes. "I'm fine."

Jordan didn't look entirely convinced, but they arrived at the nursery ten minutes later.

"Hey, Jim Bob." Ted waved as Jordan helped Jim out of the van. Ted had started calling Jim, Jim Bob, after the famous Walton character since Jim had moved here a few years ago. "You come for a visit?"

Jim just shook his head, knowing that adults, for some reason, thought nicknames were cute. Even if you were eighteen and a high school graduate. "Yeah."

Jim followed Jordan inside. Jim waved to Kelly, a summer

hire, who was ringing up customers. Jordan shouted hello to a few more of the employees as they stacked shelves. They continued to the back of the store to the office, Ted still following.

"Everything okay here?" asked Jordan as he flipped through piles of paper.

"Steady flow of people this morning," Ted replied.

"Good. Let's see, I'm going to put our Jim Bob here to work." Jordan grinned. He knew Jim hated that nickname.

"These inventory lists need to be put in chronological order with the latest one on top. Think you can handle it?" Jordan placed the stack of paper in front of his nephew.

"I'm eighteen, not eight. I can do it."

"Jordan, I need to show you something out on the floor," Ted said.

"All right," replied Jordan. "Jim, you—"

"I'm fine." Uncle Jordan asked if Jim was okay about a million times a day. *Geez, take a break, man.*

Jordan followed Ted out of the office. He glanced around the nursery. The mid-afternoon breeze blew in the scents of daffodils and roses. They passed someone inspecting his collection of bird feeders as they made their way to the bags of soil stacked waist high.

"Everything okay, Ted?"

"Oh, fine. Fine." Ted glanced around as if to make sure no one would overhear. "I know you told me not to do this ever again, but I found this woman—"

Oh, god, not again! "Ted—"

"Just hear me out. Nancy met her at the grocery store a few weeks ago. She's new in town. Single."

"You want me to go out with someone your wife met in the produce section just a few weeks ago? This doesn't give me a warm fuzzy, Ted."

"Nancy's been chatting with her several times since they met. Says she'd be perfect for you."

"I told you no the last time. I have no time for this." Then the funniest thing happened. Jordan's mind brought up the image of Kayla Jennings, the woman he'd just met. The woman with the cascade of black hair that framed her serene face. The woman who talked to Jim like a human being rather than an invalid.

How odd.

"Jordan, make time." Ted lowered his voice. "I know you've been busy this past year, especially when Jim got worse. But you need to get out, have a little fun."

"No."

"You haven't even heard what Kim's like. That's her name."

Jordan massaged his forehead. "You're slow, Ted. This is the fourth time you've tried this in the last two months. And for some reason, you're unable to comprehend the word *no*. I don't do blind dates."

"Jordan—"

"No! Now as your employer, I order you back to work." He walked away while Ted continued to plead his case.

Ted was a friend. All his employees were friends. But this was going too far. He'd been involved with women before. Some good, some bad. One really bad one, once, long ago. But his life was different now. He had the responsibility of the nursery as well as Jim. He knew his friends meant well. They were great. They'd been supportive of Jordan taking numerous days off to take care of Jim these last few months. He appreciated it. Setting him up on numerous blind dates had been cute in the past.

Not anymore.

Jim looked up from his stack of papers. "Who ticked you off?"

"Huh?"

"You look like you want to strangle someone."

"Oh. Nothing," Jordan replied as he sat down at his desk.

"Ted tried to set you up again, didn't he?" He laughed.

"You're nosey."

"No, I just know that face. Why don't you go?"

"Jim—"

"You might have fun. From what I've heard, girls are supposed to be a good thing."

"Get back to work."

"If you said no cause of me, I can spend the night at Evan's. He wouldn't mind."

Jordan's face turned from irate to serious. "It's not because of you, Jim."

It was cool how his uncle was always trying to make him feel better. He needed that. He needed that when his body betrayed him at two in the morning with mild to violent leg tremors. He needed that when he had to swallow his pride and begin to use the wheelchair. But it was uncool that his uncle didn't have a woman. That wasn't normal. "Then there's no excuse."

"What are you, my social director?"

"In training."

"Smart ass."

Jim smiled. "Got this stack done. What's next?"

"Hello? Is anyone home?" asked Maggie.

"Huh?"

"I said, 'Is anyone home?' You've been quiet since before the movie started. Then you were distant during the movie, even though it had Robert Redford in it. You know, the one you call 'a luscious piece of eye candy.' Now, I'm talking to you about Jake, and how he almost asked me to marry him, and you're off in la-la land. What gives?"

"Sorry, Maggie. I'm just tired, I guess." Kayla glanced over at her best friend. Ringlets of copper hair bobbed around Maggie's face as she scrutinized Kayla through thin-rimmed spectacles. Kayla always wondered how the spunky, go get 'em, take few prisoners Maggie Kent had become her soul sister. Kayla believed herself to be plain, shy, unwilling to take any prisoners. In the end, she guessed they found some common ground that balanced each other out.

"No, there's more to it, Kayla. Judging by that look on your face, it has to do with a man. Spill the beans!"

Geez, Kayla hated it when Maggie was right. She knew Kayla too damn well. In most cases, it was a blessing. But in this case, it was irritating. Worst of all, she knew she couldn't lie to her sister of the heart.

Grudgingly, Kayla admitted, "Okay. His name is Jordan

Michaels. He's the uncle of one of my new clients. He came in this morning, with his nephew. Actually, he didn't say much. But he has a gorgeous smile and beautiful blue eyes." Her heart beat a little faster as her description of Jordan conjured up each feature vividly in her mind. "Anyway, it doesn't *mean* anything. He's just a relative of a client, nothing more. Forget it. Now, you were saying about Jake?"

"Not so fast. I haven't seen that look in your eyes in years." Maggie put her hand on Kayla's, squeezed gently. "I know *that man* scared you years ago. I can understand your caution. But even though he was a bastard, it doesn't mean they all are. You've made sure that you kept your distance from men. I understand your fear, but it's time to take a chance. Perhaps Jordan's that chance."

Kayla sighed as Maggie's words soaked in. "I don't know about taking a chance. Besides, he hasn't shown any interest in me."

"So, show your interest in him. This is the twenty-first century, you know. Women can do that nowadays."

There she goes again, Kayla thought. Maggie, the go-getter. "I'm not like you. I wouldn't go up to a stranger and ask him out on a date, right there on the spot."

"I couldn't help it. Jake's butt looked so good in those tight jeans."

Kayla laughed. She knew that although Maggie had superficial motives the first time she met Jake Hunt, their relationship was more solid now than anyone ever expected. "Speaking of Jake..."

Maggie's face glowed as she told of her beloved Jake. "Well, I think he was ready to propose. He said he had something he wanted to talk to me about. He came over for his usual Sunday dinner. But he brought flowers and was dressed a little bit nicer than usual. His butt looked great in his khakis, by the way. Anyway, we had a good dinner, chatting about his latest article about the senatorial race. I talked about my feature article on abused children. Anyway, when we finished, he took up the dirty dishes and told me to stay put. After cleaning the table, he came back into the kitchen's doorway. All of a sudden, his eyes turned a soft brown, and he grinned. He said, 'I love you, Maggie. I—' and then the phone rang."

"Ah, so close. What happened?"

"Since he was closest to the phone, he answered it. Turns out his mother fell down the porch and broke her ankle. So he had to leave."

"Oh God! Is Jake's mom all right?"

"Yeah. Just a couple of bruises on her arms from being bounced around. It took up the rest of the evening, though. Jake's out of town now, working on another story. But," her eyes beamed brighter, "we have a date in two weeks, when he returns. He promised to finish what he started before the phone call."

"I'm so happy for you. Jake's a good man. He loves you. You have to call me as soon as he pops the question."

"Of course. Who else is going to be my maid of honor?"

Thoughts of Jordan Michaels were lost as she and Maggie continued talking. When they parted at the entrance to the restaurant, they promised to call each other in a couple days and set up another get together.

When Kayla made it home, she soaked in a warm, relaxing bath. Snuggled in her bed, her thoughts strayed to Maggie and Jake. Her heart was filled with genuine happiness for Maggie.

I just wish Cupid was a little bit more reliable with his bow and arrow.

Thoughts of Maggie and Jake's blissful happiness dimmed as sleep slowly took hold of her. Right before she drifted off to sleep, however, she thought that perhaps, just perhaps, Maggie was right. Some chances were worth taking.

Chapter Three

Jordan slept peacefully. No dreams, just a continuous stream of oblivion.

Then without a sound, he woke. He shuffled to the side of the bed and rubbed his bleary eyes. As he stood, he heard Jim crying.

It had become a routine now. Jordan had somehow programmed his body to become alert even before Jim started having an attack. He thought of checking the clock to see what time it was. But, again, he knew the routine. It was probably three or four in the morning. There was no point in checking the clock anymore.

Jordan shuffled down the hall and into Jim's room.

There was no light in the room. Jordan had learned that Jim wanted it that way. Jim didn't want his uncle to see the sickness, the tears. Eighteen was a hell of an age to begin with. Then dump a disease on top of that left your body uncontrollable and life sucked.

Jim whimpered and Jordan's insides twisted. "Jim?"

"Go back to bed."

Instead, Jordan walked in and sat on the edge of the bed. As his eyes adjusted to the dark, he noticed Jim had shoved the blanket to the floor. Curled up on his left side, Jim's eyes were shut tight, his hands clenched the pillowcase. God, there was not a damn thing Jordan could do for his nephew but soothe as best he could. He almost brushed Jim's brow, but thought better of it. Jim would yell at him. He wasn't a baby, he'd remind Jordan. Stop treating him like one.

"I'm up now. Think I'll join you, if you don't mind." Jordan hoped his voice was neutral even though his insides churned.

"I do mind."

"Well, too bad. I'm staying."

"Maybe I'll just throw you out," Jim said through clenched teeth.

Jordan knew the pain made Jim angry. He needed to take that anger out on someone. His calm, shy nephew became a fire spitting zombie during these leg tremor attacks. Jordan had almost gotten used to the insults and arguments. Almost.

"You're invading my privacy. Get out!"

Jordan did, but only long enough to retrieve a wet washcloth that he applied to Jim's sweaty forehead. Jim calmed slightly.

"Better?"

"A little."

They sat in silence a bit longer. Jordan simply bathed Jim's face.

"I feel better. You can go back to bed now," Jim mumbled.

"Okay." But Jordan stayed until Jim was asleep. He pulled the covers off the floor and covered Jim. This time, he did brush his nephew's brow. Deep even breaths escaped Jim's lips and Jordan's twisted insides began to unwind.

He considered going down and having some milk, but headed towards his bedroom instead. He climbed into his empty bed and shut his eyes, but sleep eluded him.

Tonight hadn't been so bad. There were nights when the leg tremors lasted all night. But whether they lasted ten minutes or several hours, Jordan couldn't sleep afterwards.

To relax, he thought of the other events of the day. Maybe Ted was right about going out with a woman. But when the hell did he have the time and energy to do that? It would be nice to have a female next to him, under him. He groaned with the thought. How long had it been since he'd been with a woman? When his counting started including years, he stopped trying to remember.

But as he relaxed, that image of Kayla Jennings entered his mind again. He'd studied her as she and Jim spoke the day before. She sounded as if she knew what she was talking about. She seemed willing to help Jim. And whenever Jordan spoke to her, she became shy. Imagine someone being shy around him? He was just an ordinary guy. An ordinary guy with a sick nephew, a stack of medical bills, a business to run, and a frustrated libido.

Yeah, just your everyday, ordinary guy.

Jim made his way to the living room the next morning to talk to his uncle.

Jordan had helped him get up and dressed this morning. They'd eaten breakfast in silence. And Jim knew it was his fault.

He hadn't meant to snap at his uncle last night. He never did mean it when he did. It just was so embarrassing how his legs trembled out of the blue. Having no control over your own body was humiliating. And to have a witness was even worse. The pain and the embarrassment usually blended together and he spewed it at his uncle during each attack. And Jim was always sorry for it the following morning.

He parked his wheelchair in the archway and looked at his uncle. Jordan stood at the window, the pile of papers on the end table supposedly forgotten. He looked deep in thought. Probably angry at his nephew for being such a jerk. Jim tried hard to think up something he could do to make up for all the trouble he'd been. What was it that his mother had said when Jim had first been diagnosed? The body may go, but the heart and mind stay forever. Well, he still had his mind. And he would use it to find a way to pay his uncle back.

"Did you get back to sleep last night?" asked Jim.

Jordan turned and smiled. "Didn't hear you come in. Yeah, I slept."

Jim knew his uncle wasn't a good liar. "Sorry about last night. Sorry I bit your head off."

"It's okay." He left the window and sat on the sofa.

"You going to work today?"

"I got a stack of paperwork here. Thought I'd go in after lunch."

Jim knew better. Jordan was concerned about his nephew and wanted to keep him at home a bit longer. The paperwork thing was just an excuse.

"Well, I'm going to work on the computer."

Jordan stopped looking at his paperwork and looked up at Jim. "Take it easy."

Jim nodded and turned away.

In front of the computer a few moments later, he typed in the title, *Ways to Help Uncle Jordan*. Tapping his fingers against the desk, he sat back and waited for his first idea to materialize.

Kayla took a morning break outside with a cool soda and a sinfully rich chocolate bar. A spot under a shady tree in a park next to her office building called to her, promising relaxation and peace. The mid-May breeze brushed the tree's limbs while the sun's rays warmed her enough to take off her pink sweater. Babies squealed and crawled on the grass or on blankets as groups of mothers chatted. Dabbled amongst the mothers and their babies were a few starry eyed couples. Kayla smiled as she watched one couple totally abandon their half-eaten food in favor of a giggle every time they kissed. Ah, spring was meant for lovers, she mused.

Blinking her eyes, she thought she was imagining things. But, sure enough, Jordan and Jim were coming up the sidewalk towards her.

"Good morning, Ms. Jennings. How are you?" asked Jordan.

"Fine."

"Good," Jim replied. "We went to an awesome baseball game last night."

"Really?" asked Kayla

"Yeah. We—"

"Oh, it looks like you've spilled a bit of chocolate," Jordan interrupted.

Kayla followed his gaze down to the dark spot on her pant leg. "Geez, I just bought these." She rushed to wipe it away. But her hand collided with his. He'd reached at the same time as she. Flustered, she dropped her napkin as she withdrew. Seemingly unaffected, Jordan picked up the discarded napkin and wiped at the stain.

As he rubbed at the spot, her skin underneath tingled. No man had touched her like that. Doctors and nurses throughout the last eighteen years had shoved and groped her body in a million different places. But this was all together different. Warm and gentle and pleasant. She bit down on her bottom lip to suppress a moan.

"There, I think I got it. I—" He looked up at her, and for a full ten heartbeats, said nothing.

"Thank you," she finally whispered.

As if a bee had stung him, Jordan stood upright in a flash. "Ah, sorry. I'm so used to helping Jim. I didn't mean..I meant no offense...I—"

Did she actually make him nervous? How ironic. It was usually the other way around. "Thank you," she repeated. "No harm done." Except that his touch had just aroused a feeling she thought she'd never experience. No big deal.

He stood now with his hands in the back pockets of his jeans.

Well, damn, Jim thought. He wasn't a Romeo. He didn't know about chemistry or hormones, but he knew about the birds and the bees. And although he had little experience with love, he felt the sparks of attraction crackle off Uncle Jordan and Kayla.

He'd spent hours on his list of things to do for Jordan. But now it seemed his list of a hundred and two items paled in comparison with what just popped into his mind.

"I'm having a party this weekend."

Jordan turned to Jim, but it took him several seconds to drag his gaze away from Kayla. That was a good sign, Jim thought. Of course, he wasn't an expert or anything.

Kayla looked flustered and covered the stain on her pants as if it was a hideous mole or something. "Really?" she asked, although her voice wasn't steady. Another good sign.

"Yeah. You wanna come?"

"I—"

"It's gonna be a belated graduation party for me. There's gonna be lots of teens there and Uncle Jordan may go nuts, right?"

"Well—"

"So he'd appreciate having another adult there, too,

wouldn't you, Uncle Jordan?"

"I..."

Geez, was his uncle this out of practice? "It'll just be a lot of kids hanging out and stuff. What do you say?" Jim asked Kayla.

"What do you think?" she asked Jordan.

"Uh, that would be fine with me." His uncle was so romantic. "It starts at one."

"Great. I'll be there."

Kayla and Jordan went back to staring at each other again. Well, if they didn't have the hots for each other, Jim mused, he didn't know shit from potting soil.

Chapter Four

"What the hell am I supposed to wear, Maggie?" Kayla hollered.

"Calm down, you've got a few more hours. We can get a decent, casual outfit together in that amount of time. Just chill! If I didn't know better, I'd say you were trying to impress someone."

Kayla contemplated her attire for the party. She wanted to look nice, but she didn't want to overdo it. She hadn't worried over her wardrobe since she was twelve. Now, she only bought clothes for work or jeans for at-home weekends. Flamboyant eye shadow and alluring perfume had never been on her shopping list. She'd always thought the wheelchair would scare men off. Make-up wouldn't make a difference. It was a little scary now to think that had suddenly changed.

"I'm sorry, Maggie. I…I…Help!"

"No prob. Look, wear a nice pair of jeans, your little brown boots, and your new blouse with a vest. Yeah, that's it! What do you think?"

Kayla considered. "Okay, that'll do."

"Of course, you could wear this pink blouse with that blue necklace—"

"Maggie!"

An hour later, Kayla headed out of town in dark blue jeans with a white blouse and a vest of baby blue.

She knew the address he'd given her was on the outskirts of town, but she had no idea exactly where.

In her handicapped accessible van, Kayla drove down the interstate, curiosity and trepidation beating in her heart. Leaving

Interstate 81, she turned left and traveled five miles. She turned right onto a long, gravel driveway. She followed the half mile driveway up to a beautiful, old white house, with light green shutters. Jordan's home wasn't huge, but it wasn't small either. It was surrounded by what, in her estimation, must have been one hundred year old trees. The house fit snugly, protectively, by the half-circle of towering shrubbery.

When she made it out of her van, she stopped to listen. The serene sound of birds singing filled the air. But the pleasant melody was blasted out by the eruption of music spewing at a sound decibel that would wake the dead. She followed the sound around the house, using what seemed to be freshly laid cement.

As she navigated her wheelchair around the side of the house, she came across a garden of flowers that made her nose tickle with the heavy sent of honeysuckle. She didn't know all their names, but the blossoms were made up of brilliant blues and soft yellows, deep reds and rich purples.

Upon arriving at the rear of the house, she first noticed the picnic table cluttered with the average teen diet of chips, dip, pretzels, and soda. Sitting at one end of that table was Jordan, with Jim parked next to him. Jordan looked up from his conversation with Jim as she approached. "I'm glad you could make it, Kay," he yelled above the music.

"Thanks again for inviting me. It looks as if the party is going strong," she hollered back.

She looked beyond Jim and Jordan to see a handful of teenagers milling around. Some ate by the table, some enjoyed the small pool that was at the foot of the patio, some sat on chairs, laughing and chatting.

"Glad you could come, too," said Jim.

The noise that was considered by today's young generation to be *music* ceased. As she was about to ask Jim about the vocational placement evaluation he'd taken, a guest came up to stand next to him.

"Hey, Jim, help us pick out the next CD to put on."

"Okay, Terri."

"Thanks, Jim. Hey. Pick something that isn't so loud this time," she teased.

"You got it," he said, and went off with his friend.

Jordan offered to get her a soda, and she accepted. After he returned with two cups, one in each hand, he handed one to her and smiled. Ah, that smile.

A new batch of music streamed from the stereo, but it was at a comfortable sound decibel this time. "You have a beautiful place here, Jordan," Kayla commented. "The flowers on the side of the house are lovely."

"Thank you. Would you care for a tour of the house? I'd be happy to show you. I think the kids won't miss us."

She froze. Most houses weren't designed for wheelchair mobility. Furniture was usually packed tightly together in a room, with little space in between. Doorways were too narrow for the width of a wheelchair, say nothing of the obstacle of the patio steps. But then she saw the ramp that led over the patio steps to the back door. This house had already been made wheelchair friendly for Jim, she realized.

She sighed relief and replied, "Yes, I would love to see it. How old is this house anyway?"

Kayla and Jordan were oblivious to a smiling Jim who was watching them from across the pool as they moved towards the house.

"It was built in eighteen ninety," Jordan began. "It's been in my family for over fifty years. My grandfather bought it in nineteen fifty. My father and mother lived here after my grandparents died. My brother and I were raised here."

Opening the sliding glass door, he stepped aside and allowed her to drive her chair up the ramp and into the house. Closing the door, he continued his story. "Thomas, my dear adventurous brother, didn't want to stay around after college, so he worked for a computer company that sent him on a variety of business trips. He was allowed to have his adventures and still make money." He chuckled. "I used to be like him, yearning to be adventurous. Not now. I'm more of a homebody these days."

Although Jordan grinned at the mention of his older brother, Kayla noticed the sadness that dimmed his bright eyes.

"After college, I came home to help mom and dad with the business," he continued. "I took it over when dad retired. And here

I am."

"What kind of business?"

"I own a nursery. You know plants, flowers, and the like. I used to be wrapped up in it seven days a week. But since Jim has been here, I've given over some of my responsibilities to other staff.

"So that's why you have such beautiful flowers and shrubs around your house."

"Yeah. I love working with the flowers, with nature. It must be in the genes. My grandfather started the business and it has come down the generations to me, just like the love of nature."

Beginning in the living room, Kayla and Jordan toured the house. As they moved about the different rooms, she mused that even though it was an old house, with an ancient stone fireplace and seasoned, scarred wooden floors, it had the modern conveniences of a dishwasher and an electric stove. She smiled in appreciation of how the house beautifully balanced the modern world with its ancient roots.

He pointed. "Jim's room is down the hall, at the front of the house. His room used to be upstairs, but he can't use the stairs anymore." He nodded to his left. "I created a small room off the den here so I could be close to Jim."

"Good idea."

"Want to take a break in the living room?"

She nodded and followed him.

Once he sat, he said, "Now you know about me. What about you?"

"Well, I was born in Ohio. My parents and I lived there until I was eleven and then we moved here to Virginia. I went to college after high school, and got my degree in social work. I started working for the Virginia Department of Rehabilitative Services about four years ago."

"Any family? Brothers and sisters?"

"No siblings. I think I was too much work for my parents for them to have another child." Fresh memories flashed into her mind; countless trips to the rehabilitation center, her parents rearranging their schedules for her innumerable doctors' appointments, numerous arguments between her parents.

Her parents had wanted her to fight, to be grateful she was still alive. Kayla would've rather curled up in a ball and withered away into nothingness. Her mother and father pushed and prodded, knowing, she thought now, that their endless harassment would grate on her nerves enough to get her to become part of the living again. But a large, focused part of her died that day when the truck rammed into her car. Her body slowly began to heal when she finally decided to give in to her parents' nagging. But her soul would always have a chasm where her dream had been plucked before it was given the chance to blossom. "Anyhow, my parents died about five years ago."

"Wait." He scowled, and asked, "What do you mean by 'too much work'?"

What an idiot! She hadn't meant for her insecurity to slip like that. It was easier now for the memories to come and replay in her mind, but she wasn't ready to share. Treading lightly, as not to reveal too much of herself, she replied, "As a result of a car accident at the age of ten, my spinal cord was damaged beyond repair. My legs were useless from then on and there were a lot of changes that needed to be made."

The memories, the emotions, were still a part of her, like the air she breathed. Like soiled air. Unwilling to share that, she changed the topic. "So, tell me about working at a nursery."

Was it him or did he just hit a nerve? Questions lingered in his mind, but he thought it best to wait. "What do you want to know?"

"Did you want to take over the family business?"

He laughed. "Not at first. Like I said, I wanted to travel. Backpacked through the Midwest for six months. Learned a lot about plants along the way. But the desire to move from place to place didn't last long. Too many responsibilities here at home."

"You regret not traveling?"

He thought of the time he'd spent with his parents before their deaths and the time he's had with Jim. "No."

"Do you travel at all anymore?"

"The most traveling we do anymore is out to our family cabin in the Blue Ridge Mountains."

Her features softened, and she smiled. "Family cabin?"

"Yeah. It takes us a few hours to get out there, but Jim really likes the place. Seems to relax him. I think it makes him physically feel better when we go out there. I swear he isn't as sick while we're there. Even after we return, he seems better for awhile."

"How lovely to have your own cabin. What's it like?"

"One story, with two bedrooms, a bathroom, and a kitchen. Tall oak trees surround the place." It was sweet the way her eyes lit up and the way her smile made his insides turn gooshy. *Gooshy?* God, he'd been hanging out with teenagers too long. "My mother had a garden in the backyard when I was younger."

"And did you go fishing with your dad?"

When she asked, why did it sound envious? "Sure did. You ever been out to a cabin before?"

"No."

A germ of an idea formed. "How would you—" Jordan heard the swish of Jim's wheelchair tires on the wooden floor. It was amazing what sounds he'd become attuned to in the last six months.

"Hey." Jim and Terri entered the room.

"What's up?" Jordan asked.

"We're having trouble with the stereo. Help?"

Jordan suddenly realized there was no music. Funny, he hadn't even noticed. "Sure."

They all went outside. Kayla parked herself next to the picnic table while Jordan went to look over the stereo. Within ten minutes, music was pounding from the speakers again.

"Need anything?"

Kayla looked up to see that Jordan was next to her. "No, thanks."

"Well, if you'll excuse me, I need to replenish some of this food. Be back soon."

She nodded and he left. She laughed as she witnessed a good-natured game of water volleyball in the pool.

"Having a good time?"

This time, it was Jim who approached her. "Yes. Thanks for inviting me."

"Ah, it was nothing."

They were silent for a moment then Jim asked, "Do you miss it?"

"What?"

He nodded towards the game. "To move like that."

For some reason, since it was Jim, young, harmless Jim, it was easier to speak of it than with Jordan. "Yes. Do you?"

"Oh, yeah."

She smiled at his enthusiasm.

"My mom told me when I first got sick that even if the body weakens you still have your heart and soul."

Why didn't that ever dawn on her before? "That's pretty cool."

"Well, some days I agree. Some days, I don't."

"I know exactly what you mean," Kayla replied.

Jordan was busy in the kitchen gathering food. With his arms full of chip bags and paper plates, he made his way down the ramp. And suddenly stopped. That noise. He hadn't heard it in such a long time. It was loud and warm and pure.

Jim laughed.

Not just a polite chuckle or a *hurumph*. But his voice danced up and down, just like music.

Jordan stopped at the bottom of the ramp and just watched. Jim and Kayla turned to each other as they talked, their profiles striking against the copper sky. As Jim spoke, Kayla nodded or smiled. And she always looked at him. Not around or through him, as others, too many others, had done recently. Then Jim did it again. He laughed. Jordan couldn't remember the last time he had heard Jim laugh like that, like the laughter began at his toes and gained full momentum before it rolled out of his mouth. The idea Jordan had earlier solidified.

At nine o'clock, Kayla decided it was the perfect time to leave. Jordan walked her to her van. Once she was settled behind the steering wheel, he stepped up on the foot board, so they were face to face. "I'm glad you could make it. Thanks for the company."

"Sure. Thank you for the tour."

She started the van, but Jordan put a hand on her arm. "Maybe I'm being too forward, but Jim and I are going to the cabin in a week for a quick weekend. Would you like to come with us?"

Although she would later look back and laugh at her reaction to his invitation and be ashamed of her haste to believe the worst, self-preservation was the only thought in her mind. Hadn't another man been generous to her at first, only to turn callous in the end? "Oh, I get it."

His eyebrows furrowed. "Get what?"

"You're married."

"No."

"Ha! I bet she's away on business."

"I'm not married."

"I don't—"

"You've just been in my house. Did you see any signs that a woman lives there? Any dresses, jewelry, high heels, wet pantyhose hanging in the shower?"

"No."

"I'm not married," he repeated.

She wasn't about to give up. "Engaged?"

"No."

"Gay?"

"No."

"Transvestite?"

He laughed. "No. What's with the third degree?"

"It just doesn't fit," she muttered, more to herself than to him.

"What doesn't fit?"

"The fact that you're sexy, sincere, *and* single." The words stumbled out of her mouth before she could yank them back. She glanced up to see Jordan beaming at her. "I suppose that bumped up your ego a few points."

"Just a few, I assure you. Come with us this weekend, Kay." The hand on her arm squeezed gently.

She hesitated.

"I promise to keep my ego at a respectable level."

Spontaneity was not a part of her personality. "I'll think about it."

As she put the van in Drive and sped down the driveway, she happened to catch his reflection in the rearview mirror. He was watching her. To her surprise, a part of her enjoyed the fact that he was.

Chapter Five

Ker-plump. Ker-plump.

The melody of rain dripping from the shingles of her office window accompanied Kayla Tuesday morning as she filled out paperwork at her desk. So intense was her concentration that she jumped when Jenny buzzed her.

"Kay, Mr. Michaels is here to see you. He doesn't have an appointment, but I thought I would see if you were free. Do you have time to see him?"

Well, Jim's evaluation results were in, even though they didn't have an appointment together until Friday. But, she had the time. And she wouldn't mind seeing the young yet mature man. She didn't mind at all.

"Yes. Please send him back."

She bent down and shuffled through her file drawer, attempting to locate Jim's file when she heard the door open.

"Hello, Jim. I'm glad you're eager to see the test results."

Her smile froze when she saw Jordan in the doorway.

She'd given a lot of thought to Jordan's offer to a trip to his cabin. Part of her yearned to go. Spending time in a quiet, secluded area added appeal to Jordan's offer. And to be perfectly honest with herself, she was attracted to Jordan. But all those warning bells kept going off in her head. This was so new to her, these longings and hopes. She wasn't quite sure what to do. Desire, and her apprehension of it, did a frantic tango in her heart. She swallowed hard and took a deep breath.

"Hello, Kay."

"Hello, Jordan."

Silence hung heavy in the air.

"Kay, I came to talk to you about this weekend. Do you have a minute?"

Placing Jim's folder on her desk, she turned to Jordan. Her apprehension came out in a stutter. "I—I'm awfully busy, Jor—dan. Perhaps—"

"Why don't you want to come with us this weekend?"

Her apprehension doubled as he'd gotten straight to the point.

"Let's just say bad life experiences have made me...unsure of strangers."

"Well, I can fix that." He leaned forward and stuck out his hand. She glanced at it, then up into his eyes, which seemed to be lit with humor. She stuck her hand out. He took it in his and gave it a hearty shake. "I'm Jordan Michaels. I live at twenty-three Manor View Lane. I have a nephew named—"

"Jordan, I know—"

"Jim," he continued, apparently ignoring her. "I've been working in my family business for several years now. I own a nursery, by the way."

"I know all this."

"Aha! So, we aren't strangers after all."

"That's not what I meant." His smugness was irritating.

"It seems we already know each other."

"Jordan—"

"Kay." He leaned closer, a hint of dirt and daffodils clinging to the air. "I haven't had a date in several years. It's not something to brag about. I'd never say this if Jim was here, but women, at least the women I've been with, are…turned off by him." He shook his head. "More like scared. Whenever I brought a woman home, she'd be rude to him. Not in so many words, of course. One woman ignored him, another babied him, another treated him like he was dumb. It's amazing how the wheelchair is believed to be the whole person."

"Yes, I know," Kayla murmured.

She watched as Jordan's drawn lips relaxed. "That's just it," he said. "You understand what he's gone through. You two had a real conversation the other night. And he laughed."

"Laughed?"

"He hasn't done that in months. Just a full-blown, let-everything-go laugh." He rose. "Adults rarely talk *to* him anymore.

But you did. I find that...appealing about you."

She wanted to believe him. She really did. But…

"We're leaving Saturday morning at nine. Let me know by Friday evening."

He walked to the door, but before turning it, he looked back at Kayla. "You're enchanting, Kay, and I want to get to know all of you. Eventually."

He then walked through the doorway. It took her several seconds to realize that her mouth was open and her eyes were transfixed to the spot he just vacated.

By Thursday night, Kayla still didn't know what to do.

She hated being indecisive, but this decision had too many pros and cons. Hope was tentatively budding in her heart. But hope could be easily, quickly, shattered.

Feeling like she was getting nowhere, she was saved, once again, by the ringing telephone.

"Hello?"

"Kay, he did it! He asked me to marry him!" cooed a cheerful Maggie.

"Oh, Maggie, I'm so happy for you. Tell me all about it."

For the next twenty minutes, Maggie explained, in great detail, how Jake had proposed at a quiet dinner for two at her apartment. He had brought her flowers, pledged his love, and given her a beautiful diamond ring.

"Finally, we spent the evening...celebrating, if you catch my drift."

Kayla chuckled at the glee in Maggie's voice. "Yeah, loud and clear. I'm so happy for you, Maggie. I truly am."

"Thanks." A pause, then, "So, you're packed for this weekend, right?"

Kayla had told Maggie of Jordan's offer a few days before. "Oh, I don't know. I'm afraid it's all a hoax, a big lie, like before."

There was a sigh from Maggie's end of the phone. "That was five years ago. And Jordan isn't...*him*."

"His name was Rob, remember?"

"I think Bastard of the Century would be more appropriate."

"You have a point."

"Well," Maggie continued, "maybe you shouldn't. You don't know Jordan very well."

Although Maggie had a point, Kayla was surprised by her friend's easy agreement. "Yeah. He's good with Jim, though."

"So would my Aunt Mae."

"He's a successful business man."

"So's Bill Gates."

Frustrated, Kayla searched her mind for the ultimate comeback. "Jordan's sexy."

"Two words: Mel Gibson."

"Maggie, you're my best friend. You're supposed to support me. Talk me into it."

"Why?"

"Because I want to be talked into it, you knucklehead!" And that, she realized, was the point. She *wanted* to. For the first time, she wanted to take a chance. "I want to go," she announced.

If Kayla knew Maggie at all, she knew her best friend probably had a smug smile plastered on her face right now. "I know," Maggie responded. "As my sisterly duty, I must warn you to be careful, take it slow, don't rush into anything."

"Maggie—"

"But," Maggie interrupted, "as a woman, I'm telling you to go for it, honey."

"So, your General Aptitude Test Battery scores show you have strong abilities in general learning and spatial learning. This is fairly typical of someone who's good at writing."

A half-hour into their appointment, Kayla looked up from her notes. "Jim, do you enjoy writing? Tell me the truth, since your uncle isn't here to tease you."

She seemed harmless, unlike many other adults he'd met. Harmless and funny. That somehow made honesty easy. "Okay, I love to write. Mostly stories, but I sometimes write real stuff, you know. Like journal writing. Want to know a little secret?"

"Sure."

"I have two notebooks full of my writing at home. I've just never been brave enough to show them to anyone."

"Don't worry, your secret's safe with me." She hesitated. "Jim, I'm sure you're well aware of the unpredictable nature of MS."

Did he ever! "Yes. But I want to be able to do something. I feel...useless, you know?"

"I can understand that. But we also have to work with your MS in mind. Do you find there are certain times during the day when your strength's better than others?"

"I would say early afternoons, right after lunch. But, like you said, it isn't always predictable."

"Okay. What other symptoms do you have?"

"Leg tremors are the biggest problem. Some blurred vision, but luckily not a lot." Yet. He could never decide which was worse. The symptoms themselves or the unpredictability.

"Writing seems to be your strongest ability, and there might be a possibility that we could get you a flexible job writing for a newspaper or magazine. Perhaps you could help write up the information published in pamphlets. That way you could write and still have an adaptable schedule to your physical needs. You—"

Jim yawned then grinned sheepishly. "Sorry."

"Late party last night?"

"No. Bad leg spasms. They've gotten worse in the last few days."

"I'm sorry."

"Even though I told him to go to bed, Uncle Jordan stayed up with me until the spasms stopped." They hadn't been as bad as usual, but the pain came out as a bark. At Jordan. And his uncle had simply stayed. Strong and silent. "Speaking of Uncle Jordan, have you decided to come with us this weekend?"

"I...I still don't know. I'll be sure to let you two know by tonight though."

She was hesitating. Not a good sign. "I don't know if this is my place to say, but I'm going to anyway. Uncle Jordan has been good to me, even before my parents died. Something happened to him when he was in college. I'm not sure what it was. He doesn't talk about it. Grown-up stuff he always tells me. But I think it had to do with a woman and it hurt him badly. He has dated from time to time, but nothing serious. He has never asked a woman to the cabin, and he has never talked about a woman in front of me before. Until last week, when he started talking to me about you."

She couldn't help it. She smiled.

Jim nodded, began to steer his wheelchair toward the door, but stopped. "He's at the nursery today. There was a shipment of flowers that needed to be sorted through. My friend Mac brought me here. In case you decide before this evening, here's the number."

Jim wrote the number on her notepad. And said a little prayer to the gods of love that his idea worked.

She stared at the number as if it had venom.

After Jim left, her mind raced. Did she really have a possibility with Jordan? A mixed relationship between a disabled and non-disabled person was so difficult. So many criticisms, from within and without. And what of this incident in college? Was she ready for all of this? She'd lived through so much and survived. But this?

Kayla sifted through the muck of anxiety to find desire beneath. Desire to try, desire to hope.

She dialed the nursery's phone number and anxiously waited.

"Michaels Family Nursery, may I help you?"

Heart pounding like Thumper's foot, she said, "Hello, Jordan, it's Kay. Am I interrupting anything?"

"No, not at all. I'm glad you called."

"Jim was just here for his appointment, and he gave me this number."

"Have you decided about this weekend?"

Thinking herself slightly crazy, she answered, "Yes. The answer is yes."

"Good. I'm so glad you've decided to come."

Shyly, she admitted, "Me too."

"How about we pick you up at nine A.M. at your place?"

"Sounds good to me. I've never been to a cabin. What

should I pack?"

"Jeans, t-shirts, and a sweater or two. It gets pretty chilly at night. Also, suntan lotion. If you go on the boat with us, you could get pretty burned if we stay out for awhile."

Her hands slightly shook as she wrote. "Got it. I'll be ready at nine." She gave him her address and directions.

"I'm glad you're coming," he repeated. "I look forward to it. See you tomorrow."

Listening to the dial tone, she stared at the phone. That was amazingly easy.

When realization hit, Kayla shouted "Yes!" and did a little jig right there in her wheelchair.

Chapter Six

The light breeze cooled her face and tossed her hair as Kayla waited outside her apartment building. Jordan pulled up at exactly nine A.M. Jim waved from his position in the backseat. She waved back and watched Jordan get out of the van and come around to her.

"Good morning, Kay."

"Good morning."

"You didn't have to wait outside for us."

"It was a sunny day with a nice breeze. I couldn't resist."

He smiled, took her small, leather bag from her lap, and put it in the back of the van. Returning to her, he nodded towards the front seat. "It looks like you're my co-pilot this morning. Jim's still tired, so he may stretch out in the backseat to take a nap. You mind being up front?"

"No, not at all. It'll give me a chance to see the scenery," she replied, wheeling her chair to the passenger door.

"Here, I'll help you. Just wind your arms around my neck and I'll do the rest."

She put the brakes on and lifted her arms. As he gently pulled her up, she caught a whiff of his scent, a heady combination of pure masculinity and daffodils. She could feel his muscles tense and shift as he held her. For a fleeting second, she was in heaven. His hand gently gripped her ribs through her shirt. The feel of her skin being caressed, even through thin material, sent goose bumps racing up her neck. She fought the urge to let her hand trail through his thick, blonde hair. She reveled in his touch and scent for as long as she could. But it soon ended when he lifted her onto the van's front seat, and shut the door.

Shocked by his touch, by his nearness, Kayla tried to calm her agitated system. Deep breaths, she thought. Deep breaths. She continued to breathe deeply as he loaded and strapped in her wheelchair in the back of the van. When she heard his door shut, she took in one final deep breath and turned to Jordan convinced she'd calmed herself. At least outwardly, she hoped.

"Have you had your breakfast yet?"

"Yes," she answered.

"It's a three hour trip. Jim and I usually get lunch at a town that's about ten miles from the cabin. If you get hungry, or need to stop on the way, let me know."

As Jordan managed his way out of the city and onto the interstate, she saw Jim in the rearview mirror. His eyes carried dark, heavy circles under them and his head kept nodding downwards as the car's movement lulled him.

"I need to lie down and rest for a bit," Jim finally said, giving into his exhaustion.

"Rest up," Kayla agreed.

Five minutes later, she heard a soft snore coming from the back seat.

"He slept pretty good last night, but we had to get up kind of early to pack this morning. I even offered to cancel the trip. He nearly bit my head off when I did. He can be so stubborn sometimes," Jordan said.

He smiled in such a way that made Kayla's heart melt like hot butter. "Did he get that stubbornness from you or his parents?"

With a chuckle, he replied, "I suppose it's a Michaels family trait. Thomas was more stubborn than I, so I'd have to blame my brother the most."

"Seriously, I think you're doing a lovely job helping Jim. I don't know many single men who would take in an ill teenager."

"Jim's family. Family takes care of family. I didn't get to know him until he was ten. I'd been away at college and then Thomas and Beverly lived in California until dad got sick. They moved back here to help dad and me with the business. That's when I started being a real uncle to Jim."

She was touched by the love for Jim that reflected in Jordan's eyes.

"Anyway, when Thomas and Beverly were killed last year, it just seemed natural to take care of him."

"Well, for what it's worth, I think you've done a great job."

"Thanks."

For the next hour, they talked about little things. He tried to teach her about flowers, she tried to teach him about cats.

When Jim woke an hour later, he heard Kayla laugh. "What's so funny?" he asked. As the fog of sleep evaporated, he looked over at his smiling uncle. Jim decided his plan was going good, so far. He had to make sure he took naps more often.

"Oh, good morning," Jordan replied. "Actually, we were discussing you."

"Oh?"

"I just told her about the time you decided to take a nose dive into the manure pile we had out at the nursery. What were you, nine?"

"I don't remember," Jim mumbled. Adults had the most amazing memories. His plan was working, but at much personal cost.

"So, Jim," Jordan changed the subject, "what are you writing about now?" He looked at his nephew in the rearview mirror.

Writing was a touchy subject for Jim. He was good at writing, but it wasn't, well, *cool.* Being a pilot, now that was cool. But he couldn't do that. Funny, he couldn't fly a plane, but he could write about flying a plane. It was too complicated to explain to his uncle, though. "Nothing."

"Sure?"

He hated being asked. It was private. "Have you been snoopin' in my room?"

"James Henry Michaels, don't you get snippy with me."

Ah, shit, he was in trouble. The use of his three names was a sure sign of anger. Jim glanced up to see that Kayla was looking out her window, as if wanting to hide. It made him feel worse. "Sorry. I just don't want to talk about it."

Jim watched his uncle's facial expression in the rearview mirror. It went from angry parent to relaxed uncle in two short minutes. "All right."

Thankfully, Jordan changed the subject, quizzing Kayla about the Stargrass wildflower they passed along the highway.

Soon after, they reached the restaurant that Jordan had mentioned earlier. Kayla was surprised that the staff knew the Michaels men well enough that they welcomed them by name.

As she ate her crunchy, tender chicken sandwich, steamy cheese fries, and an orange soda, Jim and Jordan ate burgers so hot and juicy that their hands were soaked by the end of the meal. After their apple pie desserts, she insisted on paying the bill.

"You're kind enough to share your cabin with me this weekend," she said. "The least I can do is pay for our lunch."

"You're our guest, Kay."

She gave him what she hoped was one of her don't-you-dare looks. She could be timid, she knew. She was also aware that she possessed a stubborn streak that popped up from time to time. And it chose to make an appearance now.

Jordan was a quick learner, she noted. He gave in and she paid the bill.

Ten minutes later they pulled up the gravel driveway towards the cabin. And, instantly, she fell in love with the place. Eight soaring, deep green oak trees surrounded the cabin. The cabin itself was constructed of dark maple, enhancing the richness of the surrounding trees. There were two steps, at least six feet long, leading up to the roof-covered porch. To the right of the steps was a wheelchair ramp, faded and scarred from frequent use. A large *M* had been scriptly engraved into the center of the front door.

"It's lovely here," she breathed, after Jordan helped her out of the van. Lush leaves swayed in the light afternoon breeze. The sun's rays trickled through the dancing limbs, scattering shadows over the cabin and surrounding land. Synthesized in the breeze was the scent of roses and lilies and freshly fallen rain.

"Yeah, I love coming here as much as I can," said Jim, who had parked next to her.

Jim's words stirred her from her reverie, and she shook her head in acknowledgement. She watched Jordan unpack the van then followed Jim up the ramp and into the cabin.

Her gaze first fell upon a fireplace, dusty and dingy, directly across from the entrance. In the center of the main room was a long, ivory white sofa that sharply contrasted the dark wood of the surrounding walls. Across from the sofa were two white, stuffed, high-backed chairs. On either side of the fireplace was a door that led into what Kayla thought was one of the two bedrooms. To the right was a small kitchen with a light wooden table with four matching chairs.

"Let me show you to your room, madam," said Jordan as he bowed then smiled.

Entering the room, she sighed with glee at the double bed with a faded red bedspread and a handmade quilt folded neatly at the foot of it. Across from the bed was a small three-drawer dresser. Atop it was an empty porcelain vase and an antique oval mirror. To the right of the dresser was a huge window that Jordan walked to and opened, causing the curtains to dance, buffeted by the breeze that drifted through.

"It's a little stuffy now, so this should help," Jordan said. "We'll close it at night because it'll get cold."

For several moments, he stood at the window and looked out at the backyard. She thought at first that he was enjoying the view. But as the silence stretched out, Kayla became concerned. "Jordan?"

He jumped slightly, as if he'd been thinking and forgotten where he was. He turned. "Sorry."

"You okay?"

"Yeah. Come here. Look."

She wheeled next to him and followed his gaze out the window. Two deer nibbled at the grass.

As if in a sanctuary, Jordan murmured, "My mother would stand here and watch these deer for hours. She'd get mad and complain about them eating her azaleas. Even threaten to shoot them once or twice. But in the end, she'd just stand here and watch."

"I can see why," Kayla replied.

Oblivious to being observed, the deer continued to munch. Their stumped tails swished, their heads rose, ears pivoted. And suddenly, they were gone.

Smiling, Kayla turned to Jordan. Sorrow etched itself at the corners of his eyes, and she realized that except for Jim, Jordan was now alone in the world. Just like her.

She looked down to find his hand on hers. His thumb stroked her flesh and her smile grew at the goose bumps that surfaced. She glanced up to see the sorrow around his eyes had been replaced by joy.

On the other side of the window, chickadees and robins sang. The fragrance of flowers and rain was stronger here at the back of the house. The sun played peek-a-boo with the trees. And Jordan finally said, "You're—" Then there was a knock on the front door.

What? You're what? What was he going to say? He felt like a bumbling teenager all of a sudden. He'd turned from watching the deer to look at her face. Her gaze was focused on the deer, her lips curved into a pure smile. And he was sure that he made the right decision to invite her here. But then he was going to go screw it up by telling her he thought she was beautiful. The poor woman probably would think he was psycho and go screaming from the cabin.

He was just an ordinary guy. How the hell was he supposed to do this?

There was another knock. Jordan sighed, squeezed her hand, and left to answer the door. He opened the door to find a slim girl with blonde hair that reached the middle of her back and spindly legs that ended in flip-flops.

"Hi, Sandy. You looking for Jim?" Jordan asked.

"Yes, Mr. Michaels. I thought I saw you guys drive down the road."

"Hey, Sandy, what's up?" Jim beamed as he made his way over to Sandy.

"Hey, Jim. Well, there's a party at Alex's house tonight. When I realized you guys were here, I thought I would invite you. Wanna come?"

"Yeah, I'd love to go. I haven't seen the gang in a month or so. And I'm a graduated man now," he said, straightening his back and puffing out his chest.

Jordan spoke up. "Well, I don't know, Jim. We have company. What do you think, Kay?" She could tell Jordan was teasing his nephew.

When she saw Jim's hopeful face, she smiled. "Go on, Jim.

Have a good time."

Jim looked from her to his uncle with longing in his eyes. Jordan chuckled. "Go ahead. Us old people will find something to do with ourselves."

Jim's face lit up again. "Great!"

A little after five, Sandy returned to pick Jim up. Waving as the two teens departed, Jordan turned to Kayla. "I think he's happy to have ditched his elders."

She laughed. "It was so obvious he wanted to go. I saw that gleam in his eye when he talked of seeing his friends. Sandy and Jim seem to be really good buddies."

"Yeah, they've seen each other a lot over the summers. She lives about ten minutes away, along the main highway. It's about time to start dinner. Why don't you help me?"

She followed him inside to the kitchen, and for the next two hours they talked about everyday subjects, such as the weather, his family recipes, and their careers. They ate outside, on a picnic table across from the cabin. Enveloped by the sweet fragrance of growing grass, budding flowers, and the steady tone of Jordan's smooth voice, she truly relaxed. Uncertainties still flickered in her mind, doubts that had their roots in the past. Jordan seemed to be a patient man, a man who listened, really *listened* to her. Some of those roots were withering away.

Somewhere, in some concealed chamber of her heart, she admitted to herself that she was falling in love with him. But because that place was so well hidden from herself, she could only identify it as a deep tug in her chest.

As the sun set and the air turned chilly, they decided to go in. She helped him clear off the picnic table by carrying some of the dirty dishes in her lap to the kitchen. After placing the dishes on the kitchen counter, she turned to go back to her room when he put a hand on her shoulder.

"Wait. I want to talk to you," he said

"That's funny. I thought we'd been talking."

He sat down at the kitchen table, and grasped her hand. She

could get used to that, his gentle touch. With his eyes piercing hers, he said, "I want to know why you're nervous around me."

She struggled to move her hand away, but was unsuccessful. She scoffed. "I'm not."

"Yes, Kayla, you are." That was the first time he'd said her full name and her heart sighed because of it. "You see, I like you. A lot. When we talk about everyday things, I feel a connection. But there's this invisible barrier that you put up, as if you think I'm going to hurt you. I can't break down that barrier until you tell me about this fear of yours." Then softly, gently, he beseeched, "Please."

A part of her said to trust him. She could see it in his docile eyes, hear it in his serene voice. The other part wanted her to withdraw into herself, within that inner sanctuary, where she knew she was safe. Safe, but very alone. Two opposing elements warred inside of her for several moments. But in the end, his gentle pleading melted her apprehension.

"All right, Jordan."

She moved into the warm living room and parked in front of the fireplace. He started to pull over one of the high-backed chairs, but she stopped him. "Jordan, if you want me to tell you all of it, without losing my nerve, I can't have you near me. Nothing personal, but you distract me. If I'm to get it all out, I need you to please sit on the sofa."

He obliged, moving to the sofa the color of freshly fallen snow.

Kayla had only glanced briefly at the fire Jordan had started earlier. But now she absorbed its heat, gaining strength from its leaping flames. As flames flickered and hissed, she found herself returning to her past. It was a visit she hadn't taken in many years.

"I guess I should begin with the accident. I was twelve, and my mom had just picked me up from school. We were almost home when a truck hit us, on my side of the car. It had run a red light and skidded on some ice, I guess. I don't actually remember the accident. All I remember is waking up and not being able to move my legs. I was stunned at first, then scared, then angry.

"When they started me on physical therapy, I refused at first," she continued, feeling twelve years old again. "I would rather lay in bed than use that damn wheelchair. But my parents kept pushing. They'd say, 'At least you're alive, Kay. Just fight and get on with your life.' I think I finally used the chair just to shut them up. So, I did what they said and buried my emotions. I just went on auto pilot. School was hell. Being a teenager is rough enough, but having a disability on top of that made it worse. I was constantly teased for being different. I had to use the school elevator and I needed help getting my lunch because the counter was too high for someone in a wheelchair. I went from being one of the most popular girls in school to being...nothing. I felt very different. I felt...wrong, I guess. I felt so alienated that I ached inside.

"My parents knew I was depressed, but I didn't tell them about the daily harassment at school. I learned after awhile that they would only tell me to let it roll off my back and ignore it. No one ever showed me a way to fight back."

Memories, although distant, were still thick with humiliation. "I had crushes on guys," Kayla continued. "Once a *friend* of mine let it slip that I liked this one particular boy. It must've gotten back to him because he confronted me in class about it. He said he wouldn't go out with a retard like me. He teased that I was probably already going out with Eric, 'the other retard.' Eric was a student in the only special education class in the whole school. Us retards were supposed to stick to our own kind, I guess. Anyway, the rumor was started that Eric and I were going out. The rumor just gave everyone something else to tease me about. I learned to never let anyone know my true feelings. I kept my mouth shut.

"This was before the current movement for independent living or the Americans with Disabilities Act."

Many other memories vied for her attention, but they seemed unimportant at the moment.

"God only knows how, but I graduated from high school. My parents were pushing me to go to college, so I did. College was not too bad, at first. There were a variety of people that went to my university. I made some good friends. That's where I met Maggie, my dearest friend and roommate. She *made* me have fun, made me laugh. And let me cry on her shoulder, too. We've been best friends ever since.

"Things were going fairly well, although I was running behind schedule. I changed my major a few times. Couldn't make up my mind about what to do with the rest of my life. But my grades were good. I was a junior in college when I hit twenty-three. I was taking an upper level English lit course when I met him."

Cold, steel animosity rose into her throat at just the thought of him. "His name was Robert Vaughn. We became friends as we went through the course together. We'd share class notes and chat during class. I had a little crush on him and was thrilled when he asked me to be his study partner.

"It was the end of the semester and finals were coming up. Rob and I were in my dorm room, studying. He asked to take a break, and I agreed. Before I could offer him a soda or a snack, he sat on the bed next to me. He suddenly kissed me. I'd never been kissed before, and it was a lovely feeling. I'd felt I was totally unattractive most of my life. It was so thrilling to finally be treated as a woman."

She felt Jordan's gaze on her, but it didn't make her feel scared or pressured. It was comforting to her that he was letting her take it at her own pace, without interruption or comment.

"He pulled away from the kiss and started to unbutton my blouse. I froze. It was as if I couldn't move. Part of me enjoyed being wanted, desired. No one had ever treated me as a woman, as a sexual person before. Not even myself," she admitted. By explaining it to Jordan now, she found herself truly understanding it for the first time in her life. The shock, the desire, the guilt.

"But then an overpowering fear came over me, and I pushed his hand away as he was about to...touch me. He said, 'Come on, Kay, have a little fun.'" His words echoed in her brain. "When I said no and slapped his hand away again, he got this awful smirk on his face. 'What'cha ya gonna do, run away?' and then he laughed. He pushed me down and was sucking on my...chest when Maggie came through the door." Disgust prickled her neck at the memory of his lips on her exposed skin. "Thank God for Maggie. I don't know what would have happened if she hadn't come in."

This time, when she paused, she knew the worst was over. The memories were still there, but they were duller now. They had been given brief life, but now could be tucked away in storage in the back of her memory's attic.

She continued to stare into the fire. Jordan couldn't see her face, but could tell from her voice that she was weary. God, the woman had been through a lot. His heart had stopped when she told of what Rob had done to her. Well, he wanted an answer and now he had one. People had misjudged her, harassed her. He glanced over to look at her again. She was a lovely woman, though. From her profile, he admired the way the flames of the fire reflected in her ebony hair. And although he couldn't see it now, he knew that her mouth was capable of a smile and a laughter that could brighten the entire state of Virginia. And the gentle way she handled Jim just melted his heart.

Being the ordinary guy that he was, he had no idea how to handle this. He knew he needed to respond. He just prayed he responded the right way. He was so inept at this.

Jordan rose from the sofa and came to sit in the chair in front of her that he'd abandoned earlier. He took her hands, and gently said, "Kayla." She opened her eyes. "You've been through a lot. I'd love to kick that scum sucker's ass," Jordan muttered.

"Maggie's nickname for him is Bastard of the Century."

"Don't joke, Kay."

"Yes, I survived a lot. I'm not an angel. I've made mistakes. But I've come a long way."

"Yes, you have." He didn't think she looked convinced.

"Don't beat him up, Jordan. I don't know if I have the money to bail you out of jail. Us vocational counselors don't make a lot of money. I would be forced to get a second job. I hear Hooters is hiring."

He laughed. Her sense of humor was priceless. But she still only saw herself as a wounded young woman. He saw her as a beautiful, bright woman. How would he convince her to let go of her version to embrace his?

His laughter died and he lightly squeezed her hands. "You need to be taught there can be joys between a man and a woman. You're funny, kind, attractive. And I'm going to prove it to you.

Beginning here and now, I'm going to romance you."

"Now, Jordan, I didn't tell you all that for you to feel obligated or sorry for me."

"Believe me, what I feel for you is *not* obligation."

"I...I'm not sure what to say."

"Kayla, don't say anything."

He leaned in and kissed her, ever so lightly on the mouth. A gentle kiss, just a simple brush of lips. But that slight touch of flesh made her giddy and weak at the same time. At that brief contact, she felt as if she would gladly melt into his arms.

"Man, I didn't know—Oh, excuse us."

The mood was suddenly interrupted when Jim and Sandy walked in. Jordan pulled back, winked at Kayla, and then got up to greet the two teenagers.

An hour later Sandy left. Jim, looking exhausted, excused himself to go to bed. Exhaustion, acute and encompassing, had suddenly consumed Kayla, too. She shouldn't be surprised, she thought. She didn't make it a habit to tell how she really felt, and she hoped she wouldn't have to wait another twenty-eight years to confess her true feelings again. But confession was exhausting.

Kayla took Jim's lead and headed towards her bedroom. Jordan followed her into her room and closed the window. But he continued to face it. "I just want to say...thank you for sharing with me this evening."

"To be honest, I somehow feel better, lighter, now that I've said it."

He turned and smiled. He leaned down for another light kiss. She was sure she had melted onto the floor as his lips softly caressed her own.

When he pulled away, he asked, "Is there anything you need before I go to bed?"

Still recovering from the kiss, she said breathlessly, "No, thanks."

"Well then, good night, Kay. Sweet dreams."

"Good night, Jordan."

Jordan left. After checking on Jim, Jordan crawled into the bed in the room he shared with his nephew. Hopefully Jim would be so tired the leg tremors wouldn't wake him tonight.

As he settled in, Jordan thought of Kayla and what they'd discussed. *I'm going to romance you.* The words had tumbled out of his mouth before he caught himself. Great! Now a man who hadn't had a date in years is going to romance a woman. This would be a laugh. But he didn't want it to be. He wanted to be serious about it. He didn't want to screw it up. Kayla mattered. There had been others during his youth that had snuck into his bed. But this time, Kayla snuck into his heart first.

The twitter of birds chirping woke Kayla up from a sound, peaceful sleep. As consciousness seeped into her mind, she remembered what happened last night; the conversation, the kisses, the promise.

Beginning here and now, I'm going to romance you.

After washing up, she wheeled into the kitchen and poured herself some orange juice. She heard footsteps on the porch and looked up just as Jordan came through the front door. When she spotted him, her blood rushed out of her veins and into her rapidly beating heart. Last night's kiss was so small, but the memory of it lingered on her lips. As he advanced towards her, he smiled a beautifully masculine smile, bent down, and kissed her, again, lightly on the lips.

He pulled back and studied her. "Good morning. Did you sleep well?"

"Good morning. Yes, I slept very well."

His fingertips lightly stroked her face. She never realized how sensitive her face could be. "Good. Would you like some scrambled eggs for breakfast?"

Disappointed when he ceased his touch, she answered, "Yes, that sounds delicious." He stood up, found the eggs in the refrigerator, and cracked two into a pan.

"Where's Jim?" she asked.

"He's still sleeping. I think that party wore him out. He needs to be careful about conserving his energy. But he's a stubborn teen. He doesn't always listen to me."

She chuckled. "Like you were a saint at his age."

He grinned in that way that made her heart skip a beat. "Of course I was."

After Jim woke up, they packed their lunches and rented a boat for the afternoon. The breeze was comfortable and the sun's rays shimmered like spotless jewels on every wave. Like sitting in a rocking chair, the gentle swaying of the boat soothed Kayla's mind. The salty sea air tickled her nose. Surprised at how much she was enjoying herself, she smiled. She noted it was an occurrence that was becoming more frequent these days. Fun, pure fun. She'd never experienced it before. Until now.

Jim observed Kayla and his Uncle Jordan. Something was different this morning. He didn't know what it was exactly, but it was a good thing. Uncle Jordan kept touching her. Just her shoulder or a quick brush of her cheek. But the way she responded, with a smile that lit her face, made Jim wonder what *really* happened last night.

"Tell us the story about you and Dad and the cow," Jim inquired of Jordan.

"Cow?" Kayla asked.

Jordan's eyes narrowed as his gaze shifted to Jim. "Thanks a lot. This is to get me back for asking about your writing, isn't it?"

Jim ignored his uncle. Instead, he giggled and leaned towards Kayla. "You'll love this one."

Jordan sat across from Kayla, threw Jim another scorching glance, and began. "All of us were visiting a distant cousin of my mom. I was barely walking. Thomas was a couple of years older. At this point, I would like to say that I only have a faint memory of this. Thank God.

"The whole family was getting a tour of the barn. Pop, who was carrying me, put me down at one point because I was antsy. I liked the cows and giggled when they mooed. I thought it funny to watch the calves drink from their mothers' udders. I guess that's where I got the idea from."

"Idea?" Kayla asked as Jim began laughing.

"When Pop realized I was gone, he went looking for me. He found me kneeling below a cow…sucking on its udder."

Laughter, spontaneous and delightful, burst from Kayla. Jim was delighted by it. And although his uncle scowled, Jim also noticed how his uncle's grimace softened as Kayla laughed. It looked as if she attempted to speak but the words were swallowed by her amusement. She looked at Jordan's scowl and shut her mouth. But another fit of giggles overtook her.

Other stories were exchanged throughout the day. About four o'clock, they returned to the cabin and packed up.

They left the cabin at five and stopped for dinner right before they got into town. This time, Jordan insisted on paying, and Kayla let him.

They arrived at her apartment building right before nine. Jordan parked the van and insisted on walking her up to her apartment. She told Jim goodbye, and then Jordan helped her into her wheelchair. He carried her bag as they entered the lobby and took the elevator to the third floor.

Upon entering the apartment, she turned on all the lights and invited Jordan in. It was the first time any man had been in her apartment.

"Where should I put this?" he asked, holding up her bag.

"On the sofa's fine."

After he put down the bag, he wandered around the apartment, looking out the windows, scanning her CD collection, and studying her computer system.

Suddenly, Sammy jumped up on the couch and meowed to Jordan.

Jordan sat down, scratched Sammy's chin, and said, "Hey, kitty."

"His name's Sammy."

"Hey, Sammy."

"Thank you, Jordan, for a wonderful weekend. I truly had a good time."

Moving from the couch, he kneeled in front of her. Gently, he cupped her face and pulled her towards him. Halfway, their lips met. The kiss began soft, as the others had been. But then he applied slight pressure to her lips and she had no choice but to open them. The soft kiss became passionate, electric. His tongue lightly probed her mouth, exciting and weakening her with every stroke. She leaned into the kiss, dizzy and throbbing. Desire pushed aside her shyness as she began to practice on him. She was never so bold, but because it was him, because it was the man who knew her history and still wanted to touch her, boldness prevailed. When her tongue entered his delectable mouth, he groaned. Sharp, fresh pride coursed through her body. She was having the same effect on him as he was having on her.

Slowly the kiss ended and he lazily pulled away.

Huskily, Jordan asked, "That wasn't so bad, was it?"

Shyly, she replied, "No. It was wonderful." That was the first time she'd been kissed like that, like being truly desired. Her new boldness awed her.

He put his finger under her chin and lifted it. "Yes, Kay, it was wonderful. Do you have plans for Wednesday evening?"

Taken aback by the quick shift in activity, it took her a moment to reply. "No."

"Well, now you do. Can you be ready by seven-thirty?"

"Yes, but what for? What should I wear?"

"Whatever you wore to work that day'll be fine. I'll be in touch before then."

She followed him to the door. He opened it and turned around. Leaning down, he proclaimed, "Let the romance begin."

Chapter Seven

It was sad.

He was thirty-five years old, a relatively healthy male, a successful business owner.

And he didn't know a thing about romance.

It was sad indeed.

It had been so much easier when he was younger. In high school he learned quickly he just had to smile and wink and the girls came to him. College was even better because there was a large batch of women to pick from. Of course, he'd ended up making a lousy choice from all those ripe possibilities. And that may have been his descent into the black hole of bachelorhood. After that came graduation and his return home. Soon after, his brother and sister-in-law returned home with Jim. And while Jim continued to get sick, Jordan's parents died, then Thomas and Beverly. During that whole time, he had fleeting thoughts of missing female companionship. But then another crisis would occur and his desires were quickly forgotten.

But now there was Kayla.

She was different. The last time he'd paid real attention to a woman, he noticed her breasts first, her legs second. But this time he'd been so wrapped up with Jim that scoping out for women was the last thing on his mind. The way Kayla smiled at Jim, the way her voice was soft and melodic like a flowing stream, made Jordan take a second look. Now that he had, he wanted more. For the first time, he wanted more than a good look and a fast tumble.

But he'd sensed her caution. And something made him ask, made him want to know. And now that he did, it felt so...huge.

She'd been through a lot. And she had a right to be uncertain. But how was he to overcome this? His mouth had spoken before his brain had caught up when he'd professed his ability to teach her the joys of romance. The last time he'd done something close to romantic, Ronald Reagan was in his first term as president.

The thought made him shudder.

"Jordan?"

Jordan looked up to see Ted in the doorway. "Hmm?"

"Had to call your name three times. You okay?"

Jordan nodded. "Yeah."

"We need some help unloading a shipment of roses."

"On my way."

As Jordan followed Ted, he was still racking his brain for romantic possibilities. He thought of asking Ted, but he was afraid his friend would leap too eagerly at the chance to help Jordan. His friend meant well, but Jordan didn't want to scare Kayla. Besides, the last romantic thing Ted had done for his wife was probably even before Reagan was president.

Jordan and Ted unloaded the shipment off the pick-up truck. When finished, Jordan counted the number of individual flowers. As he was counting, he stopped to brush lightly the dewy petals. Soft and warm. Soft and warm and wet. *Just like Kayla's lips*.

Gliding over a petal with his finger, Jordan remembered the kisses he'd shared with Kayla. The one in the cabin was meant to reassure her that he wasn't like Rob. But the kiss that took place in her apartment was pure greed on his part. The first kiss may have reassured her, but it rattled him. And he'd wanted more. And when she'd responded, he was pleased.

His fingers moved to the next flower, his fingers again brushing the petals. *Just like Kayla*.

Duh! He ran a nursery, for heaven's sake! Why hadn't he thought of it earlier? Good lord, he was out of practice. He turned to leave.

"Hey, did you finish counting?" Ted asked.

"No. But I'll be right back."

"Where you going in such a hurry?"

"Got a phone call to make," Jordan answered over his shoulder as he walked towards his office.

Kayla rubbed her tired eyes and fought back a yawn as she made another routine phone call to a new client. Dreams had slipped in and out of her sleep, reminders of Jordan kissing her. Each dream had been a repeat of the kiss they had shared in her living room the night before. And she woke up from every dream with a galloping heart and the feel of his warm lips on hers. She chided herself every time for being so ridiculous. She was not a teenager anymore. But despite personal scolding, she'd had the same dream three times the night before.

Now, slightly grumpy from only a few hours of sleep, she was trying to track down an unreachable client. After she'd left a disgruntled fourth message on this client's answering machine, Jenny buzzed her. "Kay, you have a delivery here. I'll have it sent down to your office."

"Thanks, Jenny." She was baffled. *A delivery for me?*

A moment later, Jenny walked into Kayla's office with a vase full of pink roses. "Special delivery for you." Placing the vase on Kayla's desk, Jenny winked and left.

Kayla had never gotten flowers before.

She slowly turned the vase around, inhaling the fragrance of each rose, caressing each one of the dainty, pastel pink petals. Pink, her favorite color. She retrieved the card nestled in the middle of the fragrant bouquet.

Kay, thanks for a wonderful weekend. Here's to romance! Jordan

She had to admit, if only to herself, Jordan was getting off to a great start.

That evening, while relaxing in bed with a book, the phone rang.

"Hello?"

"Did you like the flowers I sent?"

"Oh, Jordan, they're lovely. Thank you. But, you shouldn't have."

"Now that's no way to react to a man who just sent his lady flowers."

His lady?

As they chatted about Jim and work, Kayla realized how nice it was to have someone to talk to at night, someone other than Maggie. Sharing the simplicities of the day was such a luxury, she realized.

"I'm afraid I have to get to bed, Jordan. I didn't sleep very well last night, so I'm a little weary."

"Did we wear you out over the weekend?"

Smiling at the memory, she said, "Yes, but I wouldn't have changed a thing."

"Good. Neither would I."

"Sweet dreams, Jordan."

"Good night, Kay."

Tuesday was a slow day at work. Kayla caught herself staring at Jordan's flowers several times, still amazed at this budding romance.

In the evening, answering the knock at her door, she found Jordan standing there, holding a bouquet of red roses.

"Jordan! What are you doing here?"

"I thought you needed a bouquet at home, too. These were grown at my nursery. They were picked and arranged in the vase by my very own hands," he said, with that incredible smile.

"That makes them extra special, doesn't it? Please come in and put them on the dining room table."

He did just that and when he turned around from the table, she offered him a seat on her sofa.

Why had it taken him so long to figure it out? A romance was begun with flowers. You'd think a nursery owner would know that. Thank God he'd saved himself in time.

"Don't take this the wrong way, Jordan, but what are you doing here?"

There was that look of wariness again, he mused. Like he was going to take from her what she was unwilling to give. "I just wanted to see you. And to personally deliver those flowers."

The wariness slid into pleasure as she glanced at the bouquet and smiled. "Thanks. At this rate I'll have to start my own nursery."

He chuckled. "I'm glad you like them. So, tell me, how was your day at work?"

"Boring. Mostly paperwork. You?"

"Slow. We unpacked some shipments, but there weren't a lot of customers."

Her hair, silky black, was pushed back behind one ear. It ended at the nape of her neck, and it slid over her shoulders when she moved her head. There was a slight curl at the tips of her hair. It made him want to twine his fingers around that curl. "Come here."

"What?"

"I want you to come here and sit by me."

The wariness was returning. He could sense it in her widened eyes and pursed lips. Easy, boy. "I'm not going to hurt you."

"I know."

She went to him. Desire he hadn't felt in years pulsed below his skin. No, it wasn't like before, though. Before he'd been a boy. He was a man now. Whether that transformation was a positive or negative, he couldn't decide.

But he knew this time it was different, special. Slow and easy. That's what she deserved. And for the first time, that's what he wanted. But he'd been away from this for so long, how was he supposed to do it?

Going on instinct, he reached out and cupped her face. Her skin below his fingers was warm. "Has anyone ever told you how soft your skin is?"

She blushed. "No."

"Too bad. It's lovely, especially when you blush."

He leaned closer, slowly, as not to startle her. His hands slid down to her neck, his lips brushed her cheeks. "Very soft," he murmured. He pulled back and noticed how she'd gone very still. "Is this too much?" he asked.

"I don't know."

Weren't some smooth words needed now? He searched into the recesses of his memory. And all he found were cobwebs. "How about we try an experiment."

"An experiment?"

"Yes. I kiss you once. If you like it, great. If not, I'll stop. I swear." He hoped by giving her a choice, she'd be more comfortable.

His fingers stroked the base of her neck. His thumb found the pulse there to be fast.

She took several moments before saying, "All right."

He drew close slowly. His hands wanted to roam her face again, but he left them where they were. His lips brushed hers. They were silky, delicate, as he'd remembered. Just like the rose petal. He brushed over them again. The third time, he applied slight pressure. When her lips opened, his tongue found the treasure hidden inside. Her mouth was hot, her tongue tentative. But he tempted it into a dance with his. Lost in the melding of their mouths, he barely heard a moan. He wasn't sure if it came from her or him.

He didn't care.

When it ended, his eyes were closed, his head still reeling from the passion of the kiss. "I've been looking forward to that all day." He opened his eyes to survey her reaction. When she smiled back at him, he relaxed.

She couldn't help it. She had to tease him. "Really? It didn't seem like you were very eager."

He must've seen the teasing glint in her eye because he smiled and then kissed her so hard that she thought she would faint. Head spinning, heart pounding, she grasped his shoulders for balance as slick mouths devoured each other.

Pulling back, he said, "Was I more eager that time?"

"Yes."

His hands slipped from her flushed face to her warm hands. They talked about Jim and simple things, like Kayla shopping for a new briefcase and Jordan dealing with a difficult supplier. Simple conversation. It was amazing how a man could kiss like Valentino one minute and talk about violets the next.

Wednesday evening, he took her to an expensive restaurant. Although nervous because she had no experience in dating etiquette, she ended up having a wonderful time. He made her feel like a lady. During the whole event, never once did she think that this relationship was impossible or unrealistic. For once, she just enjoyed herself without analysis or scrutiny.

Three weeks after their first official date, Kayla finished eating a scrumptious meal of fresh vinaigrette salad and tender veal at a new Italian restaurant in town. As they finished their strawberry cheesecakes, jokes were shared.

Kayla laughed. "Oh, my, where did you hear that one?"

Catching his breath, Jordan sputtered, "It's been swapped for years in any men's locker room."

"I hate to hear what other stories you've heard in such a scrupulous place."

"Jordan, it's so good to see you again."

Due to her laughter, Kayla took a moment before she tore her gaze away from Jordan to look up at two women who had approached their table. Both were attractive. One must have been in her late fifties, with ghost white hair styled into a French twist and the onset of tiny wrinkles around her eyes and mouth. The heavy applications of blush, lipstick, and mascara did little to hide them.

The other woman was around Kayla's age. Silky blonde hair fell below her shoulders and, unlike the older woman, had the gift of flawless skin. Both women were impeccably dressed, with gold twinkling at their earlobes. They looked at Jordan with nothing less than admiration bordering on lust.

"Jordan, I'm glad I caught you," said the white haired woman. "You'll be set to do the Banker's Ball again this year, I hope?"

"Of course, Mrs. Tannen. I've been doing the ball for three years now. I wouldn't think of missing it."

"Oh, good," squealed the blonde. "You'll stay for the whole evening, won't you?" Kayla's skin crawled from the overly eager blonde's imploring invitation.

"I plan to," answered Jordan.

"Be sure to save a dance for me," purred the blonde.

Kayla felt her eyes slit. Images of winding the pretty blonde's lovely hair around her skinny neck and giving it a dangerous twist brought a devilish smile to Kayla's lips. Clearing her throat, she hoped to break the spell the blonde was trying to weave on Jordan.

"Oh, ladies, this is Kayla Jennings. Kayla, this is Mrs. Barbara Tannen and her daughter, Casey. I provide plants and flowers for the annual Banker's Ball, which they host every year."

As he explained, the ladies finally turned toward Kayla, acting as if they hadn't even seen her there before. In a voice that had suddenly changed from outright flirtation to stiff politeness, Mrs. Tannen said to Kayla, "Ms. Jennings."

"It's a pleasure to meet you, Mrs. Tannen, Ms. Tannen."

Casey, obviously not as willing to be polite as her mother, just nodded her head slightly. Casey's eyes roamed up and down Kayla with indisputable disapproval, but her face was expressionless. Oh, yeah, twisting that blonde hair around her delicate little neck became *very* appealing.

Mrs. Tannen said, "Well, Jordan, my dear, I'll be in touch. Take care," then turned quickly, gave a curt nod to Kayla, and walked away. Casey didn't even acknowledge Kayla again. She simply walked off after her mother.

"*Friends* of yours?" Kayla asked, unable to suppress the green-eyed monster within.

"Like you heard, I've been working for them for three years on the ball. It raises a lot of money for the children's hospital."

"Is that all?"

"What do you mean, 'Is that all'?"

"I saw the way those two were looking at you. They had the hots for you."

"Please! I just work for them occasionally. Besides, Mrs. Tannen is too old for me."

His exclusion of the younger Tannen made her suspicious. "And what about Casey?"

"She's slept with every guy in town who'll have her."

"Including you?"

"Kayla, are you jealous?"

"Jealous? Don't be absurd!"

With wide eyes and a smile that dimpled his cheeks, he said, "I do believe you're jealous. I'm flattered."

"Excuse me. Are you ready for the check?"

Interrupted again, this time by the waiter, their debate halted. With the same mischievous smile still on his face, Jordan paid the check. On their way out of the restaurant, Kayla stopped off at the restroom. Still fuming over how easily those two women flirted with Jordan, she made her way to the largest stall. She didn't pay attention at first to the chatter of two women who entered the restroom. Debating which name to call Jordan when she returned, her attention quickly shifted when she heard her name.

"What was her name? Karen? Kate?"

"Kayla, I think."

Recognizing Casey and Barbara Tannen's voices, Kayla's thoughts of berating Jordan quickly vanished.

"Well, whatever her name is, she doesn't fit Jordan," whined Casey. "I've been working on him the last three years, and I thought this year would be it. He and I would be perfect together. He's so handsome. He and I would make a most beautiful couple."

Envisioning Barbara sticking her nose up in the air as she preened in the mirror, Kayla bristled with anger as she heard Barbara say to Casey, "Don't worry, darling. The girl's in a wheelchair. You know he isn't getting any, and he'll tire of her soon. The Ball is a few months away. He'll have dumped her by then."

"But what if he doesn't?" whined Casey.

"Honey, if he stays with her, we'll just have to find another supplier for the ball."

"Mom, I like the way you think."

Kayla barely heard the running of water and the shuffling of feet as the Tannen women left. Stunned and angered into silence, she simply sat in her wheelchair as minutes passed by. Would she cause Jordan to lose important business? Even though the Tannens were, to say the least, snobby, perhaps even crude, it was obvious by their fancy suits and expensive shoes that they paid Jordan's nursery well for its services.

It was true that she and Jordan weren't sleeping together, although the thought had entered Kayla's mind on numerous occasions. She'd never discussed it with him. She didn't know how to even broach the subject. Was he sleeping with someone and just enjoying Kayla's company for the conversation and laughter? Were the romantic feelings she felt for Jordan one-sided? And even if they weren't, was she capable of making love? There were many things she couldn't do. Was this one of them? She'd always wondered but never knew.

Seeds of hope and love that were beginning to bloom within her slowly turned into themselves and shrank back into nothingness.

Pulling herself out of her stupor, she left the bathroom with a heavy heart and a sick stomach.

"Kayla, talk to me. What's wrong?"

Feigning a headache, Kayla had tried to ward off Jordan's attempt to see her to her apartment. It didn't work. Once she made it into her apartment, he invited himself in and sat on her couch.

"If it's about those two women, you're taking it way too far," Jordan added.

"I told you, I have a headache. Maybe it would be best for you to go home."

"I'm not leaving 'til—"

"Damn it, Jordan, would you just go!" Now that she was over the shock of the Tannens' comments, it was transformed into blood boiling rage. Not only at the women and their comments that had blind-sided her, but at herself for being the object of another insult. Hadn't she grown out of this? Hadn't she learned to deal with this discrimination and alienation? Weren't people supposed to be politically correct these days? Behind closed doors, there were and always would be people who thought less of her just because she was disabled. Laws could be improved and enforced, but people's core attitudes could remain stubbornly steadfast.

Barbara and Casey's unexpected comments also brought up Jordan and Kayla's platonic relationship. Jordan's kisses left her feeling breathless and longing for more. But that's all it had been and perhaps it was all it could be. Always, in the back of her mind, Kayla felt imperfect, incomplete in her own skin. No matter how badly she wanted Jordan in her life, nothing could change who she was. Realizing that, accepting that, was harder than she thought possible. The belief that this relationship would work was slipping away from her like a rope gripped by greasy hands.

"Just go, Jordan." She suddenly felt weary. "And perhaps it would be best that we stop seeing each other for awhile."

"Just because two women flirt with me is no reason to break-up, Kay," said Jordan in a frustrated voice.

"It's more than that. But you wouldn't understand."

"Then tell me. I listened before, I'll listen again."

Numb, Kayla sat there, unable to move or explain. Words were empty and ineffective in this situation. "Jordan, don't you see? I'm in this wheelchair. I can't be perfect for you. Others will think less of you because of me. You don't deserve that."

"Where the hell did this come from? I've always known you were in a wheelchair. Why this sudden doubt?"

"Let's just say I got a harsh dose of reality recently."

Bending down in front of her, he looked into her face while he caressed her hands. "Kayla, you can't be serious. We…we care for each other. I know we do."

Was that love in his eyes? Kayla wasn't sure, was afraid to know. With every moment that passed, her heart broke a little bit more. But he didn't know what he was getting himself into. And she'd been selfish for letting him think he did. On a wavering whisper, she said, "Just go, Jordan. It's for the best. Please."

"This is insane, Kayla. I don't know how to fight what's gotten into your head."

Kayla couldn't say anymore. It was done, decided long before this moment by a truck out of control on an icy road. She shook her head and pushed her wheelchair backwards, away from him. Moving towards the door, she opened it in dead silence. Unfolding from his crouched position, he walked to the doorway but turned to face her before he left. "This isn't over, Kay."

Without looking up, she simply said, "Yes, it is."

After a brief pause, he walked out the door. With just

enough effort, she shoved the door so it would latch on its own. Although she felt empty, she found the energy to make her way to the window. For interminable moments, she watched the lights of the city below. But once the finality of what had happened hit her like a bullet in the chest, the city lights blurred as pools of tears spilled from her eyes.

"Don't argue with me, Jim," Jordan yelled.

"I'm not."

"Yes, you are. Just admit you did it."

"I was not the last one to drink the milk," Jim muttered through a clenched jaw. "I believe it was you."

"Don't you think I'd remember throwing the carton away?"

"Apparently not."

"Look, mister, your attitude has gotten out of hand."

A man had his limits and Jim was reaching his. It had been a week since Uncle Jordan had turned into Mr. Hyde. And he had a pretty good idea as to why. "*My* attitude? What about yours?"

Jordan spun from the cabinet from which he was retrieving a glass. "Me? We're talking about you."

"No, it's about time we talked about you."

"Look, young man, you've been arguing with me all week. I don't know where this new attitude has come from. But it's gotta stop. This isn't like you."

"Me? Just take a moment and think. I'm not the only one you've had trouble with this week." When Jordan didn't argue, Jim continued, "You yelled at Ted for not stocking the cash register with enough quarters. You gave Jill the riot act for not stacking the pots evenly. You've bit my head off for playing my music too loud or too long. See a pattern here?"

Jordan sat down at the kitchen table with his empty glass. "Perhaps I've been a bit harsh. But—"

"Harsh? You've been down right mean. I've never seen you like that. Ever."

As Jim noticed realization dawn on his uncle's face, he decided it was time to say it. Someone had to. "Go talk to her,

Uncle Jordan."

"Who?"

Jim shook his head. He was starting to lose hope for his uncle. "Kayla."

Jordan's gaze shifted up from the table to Jim. "I just need to give her some time."

"If you give her any more time, you'll have no friends left. You'll have ticked them all off. They'll never want to speak to you again."

"Jim, you're a young man. You don't understand women. You—"

"Ah, hell, either you go talk to her or I will."

"Jim—"

"And it's lame when your nephew has to do the work for you," Jim interrupted. "Look," he moved closer to Jordan, "she means something to you. And it's driving you nuts, as well as the rest of us."

Jordan sat back and turned towards Jim. "How the hell did you get to be so grown-up all of a sudden?"

When Jordan smiled, Jim relaxed. "Oh, I've had a few teachers."

Jordan reached out and ruffled Jim's hair. "Sorry I've been such a nut."

"You gonna talk to her?"

"I'll think about it. Now go and make a grocery list with milk as the first item."

His uncle looked a little bit more relaxed now. Not like he was going to kill somebody anymore. It was a start.

Jim left. Jordan stood up with this empty glass and walked to the refrigerator for some orange juice. As he passed the garbage can, he saw the empty milk container. And then he'd remembered how he'd used the last of it up last night. He couldn't sleep, which had been the case all week. So he'd come down and had some warm milk to relax him. And had thrown away the carton himself.

Hell, it was getting pretty bad if your eighteen-year old nephew was giving you sound advice.

He got out the orange juice. And thought how best to follow his nephew's advice.

Proud of herself for holding up so well thus far, Kayla continued to enter client information into the computer. Tears had welled up and overtaken her the first three nights after her confrontation with Jordan. It was pitiful, she knew, but she was new at being a heartbreaker. It had been a week since the last tear had dropped, though. Enough was enough, and she needed to get on with life, such as it was. So no more tears, no more regrets.

Congratulating herself for being so brave, she continued to enter data. When she heard a knock on her office door, she told the person to come in, her gaze still on the screen. She completed the last sentence of data and then finally looked up at her visitor.

Jordan.

Her self-congratulations quickly faltered, tripping over disbelief and shock. All the emotions that she was confident were dispelled from her heart rushed back in. Her breath caught in her throat. Trembling hands moved from the keyboard to her desk as she faced him. Her heart ached with love and longing for him. No matter how hard she'd fought to get him out of her mind, Jordan was undeniably etched into her heart forever.

"Kayla." The one word, simply spoken, threatened to undo her. Slowly recovering from her shock, however, she did her best to hide it.

"Jordan. What are you doing here?"

He walked all the way in and shut the door without a sound. Turning back to her, Kayla noticed dark circles under his eyes. As he made the short distance from the door to her desk, she stiffened in her resolve to fight her feelings for him. For the millionth time, she told herself it was for the best.

"Over the last week, I've thought of nothing but you," Jordan began.

"Jor—"

"Shut up!"

Surprised at his harshness, her mouth quickly shut of its own accord.

Slightly calmer, he said, "Just shut up and listen. Over the last week, I've thought of nothing but you. Trying to figure out why you had a sudden change of heart, I played out that evening over and over in my mind. I couldn't sleep, couldn't think. I thought it would be best to give you some time. But someone wise told me to stop waiting. So I'm going right to the source. You're going to tell me, now, Kayla. What happened that night to make you turn me away?"

Evading the question, she said, "It won't work out, you and me. There are too many…unavoidable obstacles. You'll just end up getting hurt in the end and I couldn't stand that."

"Like I'm overflowing with joy now," he scoffed. "Wait, what obstacles?"

The anger and disappointment she thought were well buried sprang up to fuel her words. "Wake up, Jordan! I'm in a wheelchair! I can't move my goddamn legs! I can't walk with you on a beach. I can't swim in the pool with you. I can't be a complete woman for you. You act as if you don't, or won't, see that."

Quietly, he replied, "I see you clearly, Kay."

Conceding that perhaps, in some ways, he did, she shook her head. "But you don't know what others will say about you, about your family, just because of me."

"What will they say?"

Frustrated at not getting her point across, she hesitantly decided that reality was the best teacher. Taking a deep breath, she proceeded to tell him what she overhead Barbara and Casey Tannen say in the bathroom. Hoping that would condition him to see how foolhardy he was being, she stated the incident in a calm and matter-of-fact voice. After her explanation, she asked, "Now, don't you see, Jordan?"

"You should've told me."

"What good would it have done? Besides, it pointed out how foolish I was being, thinking I could be with you."

Reaching her side, he knelt down so that he was eye level with her. As his hands slowly reached out to hers, she pulled them back knowing his gentle touch would undo her. But she was wrong. She made the mistake of looking into his bottomless gaze as his warm hands softly covered hers. The love and compassion she saw within his baby blue eyes did her in. Weary, she couldn't fight it, or him, anymore.

"Oh, Jordan." She bowed her head and began to cry.

He took her shoulders and held her close. "You shouldn't have kept this to yourself. There are two people in this relationship. One can't take it away from the other. Too much has been said and done for it to just disappear."

Her head snuggled comfortably upon his shoulder, as if it was meant to perfectly fit there. Sniffling, she said, "I don't want you to be hurt."

Jordan pulled back and looked at her. "What those two said about you pisses me off so bad, I find myself wanting to ring their cosmetically altered necks. But that doesn't compare to the pain I felt slash through me the minute you asked me to leave you for good."

She slowly grinned at his description of the Tannens. He saw through their altered beauty, too. "It was killing me to do it. But I thought it was for the best."

With a voice of finality, Jordan noted, "Well, now we both know it isn't."

Kayla, once again, began to argue. There was so much he didn't understand, he didn't know. But it was quickly forgotten when his lips found hers. This kiss reminded her of what she'd been missing. His touch made her bones melt to a soft liquid. Now, with Jordan gently holding her body, her lips, and her heart, there was no doubt at all.

Chapter Eight

Kayla adorned a sweater to fight off the chilly air that crept into Duncan during mid-October. She accompanied Jordan, Maggie, and Jake to dinner to celebrate Maggie's birthday.

At the Hunter's Club, Kayla took immediate note of the spotless dance floor in the middle of the restaurant, crowded with couples swirling to Glenn Miller's *String of Pearls*. Light shimmered and twinkled off the dimmed chandeliers that hung grandly from the lofty ceiling. Candles sat idly at each table's center, giving an angelic glow to each occupant. Women wore everything from dress pants to dresses with sparkles and short hemlines. The combined jewelry of the female customers caught the mixed light of the candles and chandeliers, giving the place a cozy, romantic atmosphere.

After Maggie and her guests were seated and given champagne, they raised their glasses for a toast to the birthday girl.

"To the bestest friend I have ever had. Happy birthday!" cheered Kayla.

Everyone clinked glasses together and then it was Jake's turn. "To my future wife. I love you. Happy birthday!"

Maggie grinned and leaned over for a kiss from Jake. He then whisked Maggie onto the dance floor.

"They're a happy couple," said Jordan as he held Kayla's hand.

"I agree."

Their hands only disengaged when the appetizers arrived. Soon after, Maggie and Jake returned to the table.

The meal of steak, green beans, and mashed potatoes filled their empty stomachs. But they made room for desert; German chocolate cake, Maggie's favorite.

"That was a delicious meal," said Jordan, dabbing away the

frosting from the corner of his mouth. "Now, if the guest of honor isn't too full, I'd like to dance with her."

"I would love to," replied Maggie.

As they made their way to the dance floor, Jake excused himself. Kayla watched the crowd sway on the dance floor.

Left alone, her mind wandered. She envied the dancers' movements, their grace. Closing her eyes, she could still reach into the depths of her memory to recall the feel of her entire body moving, dancing. A small lump of sadness swelled in her heart as she watched the others, knowing she would always long for the one thing she couldn't have.

Her gaze roamed over the crowd, then focused on Jordan and Maggie. Maggie said something to Jordan that caused him to frown. Then she said something else that made him smile.

"Jordan, you're awfully quiet. Is something wrong?"

Cars dashed by as Jordan drove home. He'd been quiet, and it was her turn to be concerned.

"While Maggie and I were dancing," he replied, "she told me something. She said that she was glad you decided to come along tonight. She was worried that you wouldn't because of the dancing. When I questioned her further, she said that you used to be a dancer before the accident. Is that true, Kay?"

"Yes, it's true."

"She said you had a big dream of becoming a professional dancer. So you were devastated after the accident because you couldn't dance. Why didn't you tell me?"

His question triggered memories, crisp, brilliant and bittersweet. The feel of her body moving to the music. The amazing energy, the exhaustion of perfecting a move, the thrill of applause afterwards.

"I remember the feel of it, the perfection, the pride of great accomplishment. But, Jordan, I'm not that twelve-year old girl anymore. It was extremely hard, at first, accepting being in a wheelchair and being unable to dance again. But I have a lot to be thankful for now and I don't pine away my evenings anymore, wishing for the past." Well, that was partially true. She didn't waste her life away, but there were still moments, like tonight. Watching people carelessly float across a dance floor with no thought to how lucky they were left her with a bit of an ache in her heart.

Arriving at her apartment, she dropped off her purse and coat in the bedroom. When she returned to the living room, there was light jazz music streaming through the speakers of the stereo system. She spotted Jordan sitting on the couch, his right ankle resting on his left knee, his jacket draped on the armrest.

"I hope you don't mind the music," he said.

"No, it's lovely. But it's getting late. Aren't you tired?"

"A little. But I have time for one more dance."

Jordan rose from the sofa and walked over to her. "How do you set the brakes on this?" She showed him. And then he lifted her.

"Jordan, what are you doing? You know I can't—"

"Shh, Kay. Relax. Just hold on and I'll do the rest."

Suddenly, they were dancing. She was in Jordan's arms as he swayed to the music from the stereo. It was slow and rhythmic…and beautiful.

Her arms draped around his neck, her head rested comfortably upon his shoulder. Eyes closed, awareness of time and space ceased. Only movement, unrestrained and uncomplicated. She felt light as a feather as he slowly turned with her in his arms.

Overwhelmed, Kayla was unable to hold back the tears of joy. No one had ever tried this with her before. No one had made her feel like she did when she was a dancer. No one…except Jordan.

When the music drifted off and the DJ's smooth, husky voice announced the next set of songs, Jordan stopped. The lonely saxophone of the next song began, and he sat down on the couch. Her head still rested on his shoulder and his neck was still embraced by her arms.

"Kay?" He'd taken a chance, going on instinct again. He wasn't sure what he'd done was right. But it had felt right. When Maggie had told him about Kayla's dream of dancing, he was surprised. Kayla hadn't told him. Now he understood even more how the accident had altered her life. She had lost a dream. Something he could relate to.

Because he cared, he wanted to try and give her a bit of her dream back. But she was awfully quiet now and he wandered if he'd made a blunder. He was so out of practice.

She hugged him tighter and quietly said, "Thank you, Jordan. You're a wonderful dancer."

"I'm glad you enjoyed it."

Lifting her head from his shoulder, she smiled up at him. "I haven't felt that way in a long time."

He caressed her face and smiled in return. He hadn't blundered. His targets were outweighing his misses. There was hope yet.

She kissed him. It was the first time she initiated the contact. He appreciated the fact that she was comfortable enough to do that. And he enjoyed even more the way her mouth fit his.

When they separated, Kayla said, again, quietly, seriously, "Thank you."

"I wanted to dance with you," he said.

She smiled again. "I thought I would never dance again. But…we did. It felt…wonderful! You're an ingenious man, Jordan Michaels."

Nah, he was just an average Joe. Nothing special. He grinned, sheepishly, as she snuggled against his solid strength. His arms encircled her waist and hugged her to him.

She felt alive, free, passionate. She felt like a dancer.

Chapter Nine

At the beginning of November, Kayla was surprised one evening when Jordan showed up unannounced on her doorstep with a video and a bottle of wine. Actually it came about as a result of Jim's nudging. But Jordan kept that to himself. It wouldn't look good. *I'm so inept at this that my nineteen-year old nephew had to talk me into it.* Yeah, real good.

With her defenses slowly dissolving, Kayla felt comfortable with Jordan now. It pleased him. Each kiss they'd shared he felt her defenses against him dissolve. And although that cheered him, it left him as randy as a stud surrounded by a mare in heat. He'd tried to hold his hormones at bay, but it was becoming more and more difficult.

Her head rested on his shoulder as the ending credits of *To Kill A Mockingbird* flashed on the screen.

She said, "I've seen the movie a hundred times, but I still love watching it."

"Yes, it's one of the classics."

"Thank you, Jordan. It's been another wonderful evening."

He lowered his head and kissed her. When he pulled back, he said, "Kay, I want to make love to you."

It slipped from his lips before he could take it back. He hadn't meant to verbalize it. God knows his body had been telling him it was time months ago. But she needed time, he knew. She also needed to know how he felt. He mentally crossed his fingers for luck. He wasn't good at this anymore, he knew.

Kayla's passion quickly shifted to panic at his out-of-the-blue statement. But he lifted his finger and placed it across her lips. "Before you get that frightened look in your eyes, hear me out."

Still taken aback, she did her best to calm herself. Jordan had been a perfect gentleman since they had met seven months ago. It was an automatic response for her to tense, to prepare for scrutiny and teasing. But she forced herself to relax because it was Jordan now, and no one else.

"I'm telling you now, so you have time to get used to the idea," he continued. "I don't plan to rush into bed tonight, although I wouldn't argue with you if you begged me to. And I believe you want me, too. I want to make love to you because I want to, not to hurt or insult you in any way. When we make love, you'll learn the difference between what you experienced before and real lovemaking."

Absorbing his words, she pulled away from him and looked into his eyes. Lord, almighty, he was telling the truth!

"I…I'm not quite sure what to say, Jordan. I've thought about sex. I wouldn't be a woman if I didn't. But, to have it actually happen is a different thing entirely. I don't know what to say."

"I thought you would need time. That's why I said something now. I'll show you how making love is supposed to be."

Needless to say, it was difficult for Kayla to sleep that night.

The following morning, she called Maggie for an emergency sister meeting.

Upon Kayla's explanation for the impromptu meeting, Maggie asked, "And you said yes, right?"

"I didn't know what to say. I was so shocked."

"Why were you shocked? It's so obvious he loves you. Making love is a natural result of that."

"You think he loves me? I don't know. He's never said it."

"Probably because he doesn't want you to run away."

"What should I do?"

"Sweetie, that's up to you. But I can tell you from personal experience, making love is wonderful. It's nothing to be ashamed of. It's a beautiful thing when the two people involved want it to be."

Maggie was right, of course. Kayla wanted Jordan to touch

her. The thought of it made her head spin and her heart thump. But she felt extremely self-conscious. Her body was undesirable. How could anyone else see it differently?

God damn it! He'd really screwed up now!

He hadn't meant for his wish to slip out like that. Kayla looked at him like he'd shot her. The blood quickly drained from her face. His shoulder had been warm from her head resting on it until she snapped it up to stare at him with mortification. The sweet warmth had quickly vanished.

There was a time when that request, spoken with a glint in his eyes and a devilish grin on his face, would have won a woman over in thirty seconds flat. There'd been Vanessa Miller, with the long legs that went on for miles. And, God, Jackie Harris his freshman year of college. The woman taught him stuff that still made him blush today.

But it was different now. Kayla was different from Vanessa Miller and Jackie Harris and others. Kayla was sexy without trying to be. Her laugh made his heart sigh. When he kissed her, he could sense the boldness beneath her shyness. He wanted to bring that out in her. He wanted…all of her.

But the ladies man of his youth was gone. He wasn't quite sure who was in his place now.

He needed to apologize. He guessed that was the first step. Maybe more flowers. No, he'd done that already. Candy was too lame. And from what he remembered of Kayla's shocked expression, flowers and candy wouldn't help. Apology was the only priority.

The phone rang. Jordan moved from staring out the den window to the phone on his desk. "Hello?"

"Hello, Jordan."

"Kayla." Relief loosened his knees. He had to sit down.

"I've been thinking about what you said last night. We need to talk."

Indeed they did. But an apology over the phone was lame, too, just like the candy idea. "I'll be right over."

"You don't have to come over now. I thought this weekend—"

"We must discuss this face to face. Jim's spending the night at a friend's house, a friend he made at a writing group. I'll let Jim know where I am, but I want to come over." *Needed* to come over. *Needed* to explain. "Okay?"

There was a pause that seemed to drag on forever. Finally, she responded, "Okay."

Jordan hung up and then dialed. "Hello. Is Jim there? This is his uncle."

Jordan waited while Jim was tracked down. *What do I say? Jim, I'm going over to Kayla's to get laid. Finally.* Definitely not. *I'm just going for a visit to Kayla's. Just a visit.* Too defensive. *Jim, Kayla and I—*

"Hello?"

"Jim, it's your uncle."

"What's up?"

"I'm going over to Kayla's." Jordan read off Kayla's phone number. "I just wanted to let you know where I was."

Jim smiled. "Going to Kayla's?"

"Yeah. You doing okay? Feeling all right?"

Jim never felt better. "Is Kayla okay?"

"Yes. Why do you ask?"

Jim smiled again, but tried to keep his voice serious. "Just trying to figure out why you suddenly need to see her. Thought she was sick or somethin'."

"We're just going to…talk."

Jim was betting that his uncle was squirming on the other end of the phone. Jim smiled. "Talk? Can't you talk on the phone?"

"Look, Jim, we're—"

"Hey, Jim, mom needs the phone."

Jim glanced up to see Todd next to him. Sorry the torment to his uncle had to end, he nodded to Todd. "I gotta go. Todd's mom needs the phone."

"Hey, you never answered my question. You feeling okay?"

"I feel fine. Tell Kayla I said hello." Jim disconnected the cordless phone and handed it to Todd.

"Everything cool with your uncle?" Todd asked.

"Yeah." More than cool. His uncle might get lucky tonight. It was about damn time.

An hour later, Kayla opened the door to find Jordan on the other side. His hands were in the back pockets of his jeans, like the day at the park. Like he was guilty of something. "Come in."

She followed him to the couch. His hands weren't in his pockets anymore. But one thumb drummed against his leg.

They both spoke at once.

"Kayla, I'm—"

"Jordan, I—"

They stopped to laugh.

"What do you want to say?" Jordan asked.

As nervous energy skipped up and down her spine, she admitted, "I had it all planned out, but now that you're here, it's jumbled up in my mind."

"I'm not in a hurry. We have all night."

Kayla took a deep breath. "I've never made love before, so I'm nervous. Hell, scared."

"I've told you before, Kayla, not to be nervous with me."

She smiled slightly, reassured. But the past still lingered. "You don't understand. I don't know if I can." Jordan opened his mouth, but she leaped forward so as not to lose her nerve. "The accident left me unable to move my legs. But, it could have damaged more than my ability to move my legs." After a pause, she asked cautiously, "Do you understand?"

"You mean, you aren't sure if you can make love, is that it?"

"Yes."

Embarrassment heated her cheeks and dried her mouth. All her doubts and insecurities flooded back to her mind. She felt like she was in junior high again, hearing the words of those who mocked her. She felt the old, yet very familiar pressure to hide, to be obscure.

He put a hand on her arm, and her gaze returned to his.

"There are many different ways to make love, Kay. I can see the fear in your eyes. I'm not here to make fun of you. I'm here to love you." He began to stroke her hair. "No one else is here but me. All I need to know right now, is do you *want* to make love with me?"

Without her usual hesitation, she responded, "Yes, Jordan, I do."

Jordan smiled then, and kissed her hand. "I can understand why you're nervous. But you'll be fine with me. We can find ways to please each other. Let me show you."

She shook as fear, love, and hope swirled within her.

"Right now, all I want to do is hold you," Jordan continued. "Is that okay?"

It surprised her, his asking. Nothing forced, nothing demanded. "I would like that very much."

He lifted her up and onto his lap. And true to his word, he just held her. She'd always wanted to be held like this, no pressure involved, only the feeling of comfort that is given between a man and a woman. She relaxed, her head fell upon his shoulder and her hands absorbed the steady beat of his heart. They sat quietly like that for what seemed like a luxurious lifetime.

After awhile, she realized he was allowing her to set the pace. Although it seemed impossible, she loved him more for it.

"Jordan?"

"Um?"

"I want to kiss you."

Jordan pulled back and grinned at her. He leaned over and gave her one of those soul shaking kisses. And she gave back as much as she took.

He pulled back slowly from the kiss, and said, "This is your last chance to say no. I would be disappointed if you did, but I won't force you. You need to be comfortable…"

She placed her finger upon his lips to silence him.

She could see that his eyes were intent and full of fire. As she looked deeply into those dark, passionate eyes, she learned to trust her own feelings. Before, she'd been taught to ignore them, to lock her feelings in an imaginary cocoon somewhere deep inside herself. With Jordan's gentle words, that cocoon was slowly unraveling. "I want this. I want you, Jordan."

Her world tilted all of a sudden as he lifted and carried her to the bedroom. It steadied again as he stopped and found the light switch. The bed dipped under their combined weight as he placed her on the bed and sat down next to her. Caressing her face, he kissed her, lightly, softly. When he pulled away from the kiss, he leaned over and began caressing her neck with his lips, tickling and teasing as he went.

Her hands slipped under his sweater, and her fingers tingled as they discovered the tight lines of his muscled chest. He groaned happily as she lightly touched his nipples.

"Jordan, I want to take your sweater off."

He pulled back and lifted his arms. With only minimal difficulty, she removed his sweater. Her eyes returned to his chest to see what her hands had discovered only moments before. The sight of his chest, sprinkled with light brown hairs, made her fingers tingle with need to touch him again. But first she looked up into Jordan's eyes and smiled. "You are beautiful."

He leaned over and kissed her again. Harder, stronger this time as his lips took possession. As her heart began to rapidly beat, he pulled her t-shirt out of her jeans and over her head. Then he lowered to kiss the top of her breast that was exposed above the lace of her bra. She lost her breath as his lips showered her skin with dewy kisses. After bathing the top of one breast, he moved to the other, giving it the same thorough treatment. His arms went around her and unhooked her bra. She was then exposed to him.

Pulling back, his gaze bore into her. "You're beautiful, too."

Her blood raced to her skin's surface in a full body blush.

He picked her up and laid her down at the head of the bed. Her skin tingled as she fell upon the coolness of the pillows. He pulled the blanket back, so all she felt beneath her were the sheets. He leaned over her and began a trail of warm caresses with his lips from her neck to her belly. Her hands trailed imaginary paths along his shoulders and back, slowly learning his curves and his texture.

When he stopped at the top of her jeans, he looked up and asked, "Ready?"

“Yes,” she quietly, but confidently, replied.

He unsnapped and unzipped her jeans. He moved them down off her legs and threw them on the floor, with the rest of the clothing. Then he slid a hand under the top lace of her underwear and took it down and off her. Suddenly, she was totally naked. As the cool air made contact with her entire body, her nerves jolted. Another part reveled in his scrutiny of her body. She didn’t realize it was possible, but she marveled at how Jordan’s eyes got darker.

“Your turn, darling,” she said, coaxing him to finish undressing.

Jordan finished in a flash and returned to lean over her.

“I love you, Kayla. You need to know that, before this goes any further.”

She couldn’t hold back the tears that sprang to her eyes. “I love you, too, Jordan.”

Slowly wiping the tiny tears, he kissed her, drawing her attention back to passion. He covered her, and she felt the exquisite sensation of his rough, taut skin caressing her soft, sensitive flesh. After he left her lips, he ventured back down to her nipples, taking one, then the other, into his mouth. She tried to suppress a groan as his hot, wet mouth moistened her nipple.

“Don’t worry about making noise, darling. It’s okay.”

When he reached out with his hand and touched her intimately, she couldn’t have suppressed her groan if she wanted to. It felt as if she were on fire. Liquid heat rushed toward her center. “Oh my God,” she moaned.

He stopped and looked up at her with concern. As her eyes fluttered open, she saw his worry. “It’s okay. I…I can feel myself react to you…on the inside,” she stammered, awed and thrilled. Such sensations were new, scary, and yet welcomed.

Smiling, he continued to stroke her tenderly, giving her time to adjust to this new sensation. Fire ran through her veins as he touched her legs and kissed the inside of each calf. In the process, he delicately moved her legs. Then he made his way back up to her mouth, melting her with another passionate kiss.

“I moved your legs, Kay. Are you comfortable?”

She was touched by his concern for her comfort. “I feel fine.”

While their lips melded together again, he entered her swiftly.

He became her and she became him.

Pain and pleasure mingled together, bringing bittersweet tears to her eyes. Although she felt the pain of his entrance, she was also pleased that she could actually feel it. She thought she never would.

Jordan was still, although she saw with amazement that his eyes held restrained passion. For her.

"Kay?" he asked softly.

"Please don't stop."

The lines of concern along his face smoothed out. He began to move inside her. He kissed her, distracting her from the initial pain. Pain dissolved into desire as he continued to thrust. Her body tightened, quivered, tightened, quivered. At the peak, she cried out her pleasure with sobs and moans. He moaned too. Then, in a hot rush, his seed poured into her.

He withdrew slowly, hoping to not cause her more pain. His gaze roamed her face. Her eyelids were closed, her breath ran hot and heavy through her parted lips. The pulse at the base of her neck raced.

From the looks of it, she was satisfied. As was he.

He lay on his back and slipped his arms around her to bring her close. But he realized she could only move half her body. He leaned over and pulled her legs toward him. He laid back down, her head now on his shoulder. Her hands caressed the area above his chest as his heart rate slowed to normal. Her warmth, her touch soothed the concerns he'd had. All the times with other women had been fast. Satisfying, but fast. With Kayla, it was slow. Deliciously so. At first he took it slow because he wasn't sure of her physical condition. He didn't want to make the wrong move and hurt her. He tried to take it slow so he could enjoy her, learn her, appreciate her. But passion had overtaken him and he went on instinct.

Her fingers continued to entice his skin, but she'd said nothing yet. After a few moments, he asked, "Are you okay?"

"No."

Ah, hell, he'd hurt her. He turned and lifted himself onto one elbow. He berated himself. He'd been too rough. He knew it.

He—

His self-scolding ceased when he saw her smile.

"I'm not okay. I'm terrific."

He leaned down, lightly kissed her brow, her lips. "That was pretty terrific."

She sobered, and said, "Yes, it was."

"Are you in pain?"

She blushed and lowered her eyes.

It was refreshing to see someone blush over sex. All the past women had been experienced before they'd entered his bed. Shyness was not an issue for them. For Kayla, it was. And it probably went deeper than just him and her. It went back to a little girl who'd been robbed of a dream.

He put his finger under her chin and lifted it until her eyes met his. "After what just happened, you shouldn't be embarrassed with me."

"A little, but I'll be all right. Just hold me."

He caressed her cheek. Her face, her body glowed. It staggered him. "I love you."

"I love you, too, Jordan."

Someone else's deep breathing. Kayla heard the foreign sound as she woke from a deep, sound sleep. Her eyes drifted open, focused, and she realized the room was still flooded with light. As her mind cleared, her memory returned. Memories of making love to Jordan tickled her heart and curved her lips into a purely satisfied smile.

She heard the deep breathing cease and turned from her side to her back. Jordan was on his side, facing her, his chin resting on his taut arm, his bright eyes open. She smiled at him.

He smiled in return. "Good morning," he said, his voice deep and groggy from sleep.

"Hi."

His warm hand felt soothing to her cool skin as he caressed her stomach and leaned up on his other arm to look over her. "How do you feel this morning?"

"I feel wonderful," she replied.

"No pain?"

Although she thought she would be embarrassed at the mention of their joining, she didn't. "A little, but I'll be fine soon."

He encircled her in his warm embrace, again aiding her by gently pulling her legs over to his side.

After some moments of silence, he said, "Kay, you're awfully quiet. Please tell me you don't have any regrets."

It was her turn to lean up on her arm and peer into his eyes. She was shocked to discover that his eyes were concerned, nervous, anxious for her answer. "Jordan, I can say with all honesty that I have no regrets. Last night, before you arrived, I thought I might have regrets in the morning."

His eyes narrowed in puzzlement, so she explained. "One of the many drawbacks of being in that wheelchair is that I'm not treated like a woman. I'm not seen as a sexual person. I'm just this cute little robot in the wheelchair. And since I already believed relationships were cruel and painful, I just let other people's views of me become my own. If I'd continued to believe those views, I would've regretted what happened last night."

As she continued to look into his eyes, she lightly stroked his cheek with her free hand, enjoying the light scratch of stubble against her skin.

"But then you came along and treated me like a woman. You talked to me as though I was a woman, you listened to me as though I was a woman, and you touched me as though I was a woman. I may blush as I say this, but you awoke those sexual feelings in me that had been buried years ago."

Waiting for his response, she hoped that this time, *this time* it would be different. No ridicule, no jokes, no regrets over sharing the deepest part of herself with someone else.

He placed his hand on top of hers, picked it up and brought it up to his lips to kiss it, leaving her skin tingling. His intense eyes then moved up to look upon her. "You're definitely a woman, Kayla Jennings. And a very beautiful one."

With that said, Kayla knew there would never be another in her heart or soul. Ever.

Because words just didn't seem like enough, she simply

leaned down and kissed him. Energy, wild and untamed, flowed between them as their mouths linked passionately together. She was sharing not only her body but her soul.

She pulled herself up to a sitting position next to Jordan. Feeling physically and emotionally strong, she grew giddy with the need to be the aggressor. She moved her legs to kneel next to him. Bending over him, she began to caress his chest. She did it slowly, retracing the patterns that she'd learned only a few hours before. The sudden freedom of abandonment licked at her mind.

Her fingers drew lazy circles on his chest, making him dizzy with need again. The need tripled when her lips sought and devoured his nipples. Her tongue whipped around them and he moaned from the torture. For someone who was so inexperienced, she learned quickly. He said a silent prayer of thanks for that.

Her lips ceased the torture only to increase it by moving her hands downward. He grabbed them before they found their destination. "You can touch me wherever you like, darling. But, if you go any further, you should know that it won't end there. It won't end until I've had you once again. Are you ready?"

Kayla smiled at Jordan. "I want you to make love to me again, Jordan."

He sprang up and kissed her in a bold and unashamedly carnal mix of lips and tongues. Covering her again, he devoured her slowly, as she'd done to him only moments before. He kissed every inch of her, lapping up the taste and scent of Kayla. She responded by groaning out his name.

She finally demanded, "Take me, Jordan."

He returned his mouth to hers, and then entered her. The heat she offered, he gladly took. He moved even faster this time, letting his longings take over. Her heat was too sweet for him to take it slow. Sweat poured over his skin. Slowly, heat rose to meet heat as Jordan reached his peak, spilling his seed into her as she tightened around him.

Chapter Ten

Thinking was like breathing. Kayla couldn't turn it off. Thinking could be depressing, dreaming of impossibilities, of hopes gone unrealized. But like holding her breath, she could only stop for a brief amount of time.

Kayla did her best thinking in the morning, often waking up before the alarm went off. Thoughts of mundane things, such as work, errands, or the cat would pop into her mind. Sometimes more profound topics would be mentally analyzed, such as a specific conflict at work or a missed opportunity in her life. That's how she dealt with life's twists and turns. Take in, ponder, analyze, accept, move on.

The morning after making love with Jordan again, the pattern changed.

Instead of thinking, analyzing, solving, she simply *felt*.

As consciousness pulled her from sleep, she slowly recognized the tingle that pulsed along her skin. From her toes to her eyebrows, her body hummed. Waking up more, she took notice that her breasts were gloriously tender from being slowly suckled and lovingly nipped. Her lips, swollen from never-ending kisses, curved into a smile. Her center, although tender, was free.

Still high on memories, she turned towards Jordan. Her alarm went off. She quickly reached to turn it off, then turned back to her lover.

Lover! I have a lover!

It was the first thought of the morning.

Eyes closed, deep even breaths escaped his slightly parted lips. She tentatively fingered the hair covering his forehead, enjoying the silky feel of the blonde strands. Caressing his cheek, she whispered, "Jordan."

Eyelids fluttered until those shimmering blue eyes were

fully open and focused.

"My alarm just went off. I've got to get ready for work."

Leaning over her, he placed a delicate kiss on her still smiling lips. "Sure I can't talk you into calling in sick?"

Her second coherent thought of the day was of taking him up on his offer. But practicality won out. "It's a wonderful idea, but I need to go in today. Big meeting."

"Then let me drive you."

"All right."

After she showered and dressed, she went into the kitchen where Jordan was at the stove, making breakfast.

"You like your eggs scrambled, right?" he asked.

"Right."

Watching him in her kitchen, she began to feel oddly embarrassed. Only a few hours before they'd both been totally naked, loving each other. Now they were fully clothed, talking about breakfast, a purely commonplace event, and she felt timid.

Damn, she was starting to think again!

As a distraction, she fed Sammy while Jordan made breakfast.

They sat at the table, only the clang of silverware against stoneware accompanied their meal. Kayla wasn't sure if Jordan was quiet because he had second thoughts about last night or he was wondering about Jim or for some totally different reason. When she'd finished eating, she looked up to catch him looking at her.

"I was thinking of picking you up from work this evening and having you come to my house for dinner," he said.

So, it was a totally different reason, Kayla thought. She wasn't sure what she was supposed to say the morning after. For all her years of constant thought and planning, she'd never thought of a morning like this. Her voice was timid when she answered. "That would be fine with me."

"Kay, is there something wrong?"

"No—Yes—Maybe." Mad at herself for her own indecision, she scowled at her eggs.

"You said this morning that there were no regrets. Have you changed your mind?"

Images in her mind of them making love, her scowl bloomed to a smile. "No, no regrets, Jordan. I meant what I said before. But I'm not sure what to do or say now. Things feel very different."

"Yes, things are different now. Better, I think."

His steady voice reassured her, relaxed her. "All right, Jordan." She changed the subject. "So, what's for dinner tonight?"

When Jordan dropped her off at the front door of her office building, he helped her out of the van and into her wheelchair. Turning towards the building's entrance, he stopped her, leaned down, and gave her a kiss. "Have a good day. I'll be back at five thirty."

It took her a full thirty seconds to recover from the public display of affection, and then she said brightly, "I look forward to it."

"What did Jim say when you saw him this morning?"

On their way to Jordan's house for dinner, Kayla felt confident to voice her concern about Jim's reaction to her and Jordan being together. She was sure that Jim had figured what had happened last night. Although Jim was not Jordan's biological child, he placed highly in Jordan's heart. Jim's response to their new relationship would count heavily, she knew.

"He said hello, asked how I was, how you were, and then proceeded to tell me about a writing idea that he and his friend Steve were developing. You were nervous about his reaction. To us, I mean. Weren't you?"

Geez, he was getting as good as Maggie at being able to read her mind.

"Yes," Kayla replied. "He means so much to you. I can tell whenever you two have your little spats or by the way that you sit up with him at night when he has a relapse. You love him dearly. His response to us being together would be important to you."

Jordan placed his hand on her leg and gave a gentle squeeze. "Yes, I love him. I loved his father very much, too. I lost Mom and Pop, then Thomas. And Jim's illness has gotten worse."

Kayla heard the pain in his voice and saw it etched on his somber face. He didn't mention the incident that happened during his years at college, though. She'd hoped he would reveal to her whatever had happened to him. She placed her hand over his and squeezed it back.

"But all that pain is behind me," Jordan continued. "And now I have Jim and you. I love you both and I think you both will love each other somewhere down the road."

He gently squeezed again and let go as he turned off the highway and dodged traffic to his house.

A little disappointed that he didn't open up more to her, she decided not to push it. So much had happened already. When the time was right, she hoped he would share with her.

Jim heard his uncle's van approach. He quickly saved the work he was doing on the computer and went to the window. Jim spied his uncle assisting Kayla out of the van. When she was out of the van, his uncle bent down to kiss her. Jim grinned. When he also spied the smile that lit Kayla's face, Jim slapped his hands together.

James Michaels, undercover Cupid.

He continued to watch them as they approached the house. But he returned quickly to his computer as soon as he heard the door open.

Feigning his lack of interest, Jim began to tap at the keyboard as they entered the living room.

"Hey, Jim," Jordan said.

Jim glanced up. His uncle's face was lit up like a Christmas tree as his hand rested on Kayla's shoulder. But the smile that had brightened Kayla's only a second ago was dim now. Apprehension had taken its place, Jim noted. He wanted her to smile again.

"Hello," Jim said to Kayla. "I know that rap music isn't your favorite. So you wanna listen to some classical music while Uncle Jordan makes dinner?"

The worry slipped away into a smile when she replied, "Yes that would be great."

She offered to help with dinner, but Jordan declined. She and Jim sat in the living room while Jim told her of the new story idea he was working on. Pleased that he was telling her, Kayla listened with acute interest. He'd seemed opposed to discussing his work several months ago, but she now saw only eagerness in his expression as he chatted away. Jordan was absolutely right. She was growing to love Jim, too.

They had a delicious meal and then finished the evening with a game of cards. Eventually, Jim yawned and excused himself to go to his room.

Kayla and Jordan sat on the couch in the living room. Sitting on his lap, she nestled her head on his shoulder, enjoying the rise and fall of his chest as he breathed.

"You were right, Jordan. I'm starting to love that boy very much. He shared his book idea. And it's a good one."

Jordan held her a little tighter, and said, "He's fallin' for you too, darling."

He then turned his head and bent down to kiss her. From only one kiss, her senses began to throb.

"It's Friday night. Spend the night here, Kay. Please."

"What about Jim?"

"His room is at the other end of the hall, so if you make a lot of noise, he won't hear it."

He was trying to get her mad, she knew, and it was working. "Me? As I recall from last night, I wasn't the only one making noise, *pal*!"

He let the smile spread to a full grin. "We'll see about that."

He picked her up and carried her around the house, as they turned off lights and pulled down shades.

He turned right suddenly, walking towards Jim's room.

"What are you doing?" she asked.

"I want to check on Jim. He looked pretty tired tonight at dinner. I want to make sure he's okay."

Shocked, to say the least, Kayla began to protest. If Jim saw her in Jordan's arms, he would know that she was going to bed with Jordan. Jordan didn't seem the least bit concerned, however.

Jordan opened Jim's bedroom door. The room was dark, but the moonlight lit up the room enough to see Jim wrapped up in his bedspread, eyes closed shut. Light snoring echoed off the pale walls. Jordan slowly closed the door and proceeded down the hall.

Chapter Eleven

The fragrance of lilies and the softness of the bed of emerald grass lulled her to stay a bit longer. This place of comfort and hope begged her to settle in for a longer visit. But amongst the lilies and the sunshine, she heard the distress of a boy.

When she first woke, the false sense of daytime lingered until the darkness overtook it. Then she heard the cry again. More like a wounded animal than a human cry.

She sat up. Her eyes adjusted and she realized she was naked, alone. And in Jordan's bed.

The moan came again and she recognized it as Jim's. Fumbling, she found the switch on the lamp next to the bed. Scanning the room, she found Jordan's shirt at the end of the bed and put it on.

She spotted her wheelchair on the other side of the room. She smiled. They'd been in such a hurry to lie naked together that he'd plucked her from her chair before she'd gotten the chance to speak.

She heard Jim again and the sound yanked at her heart.

"Jordan." Having no choice, she called out to him. She wanted to get to Jim, but couldn't without her wheelchair.

"Jordan."

He came into the room as she was about to call out a third time.

"I'm sorry." He sat on the bed next to her. "He didn't mean to wake you up."

"What's wrong with him?"

"Leg tremors. He's been on medicine for awhile now. It seemed to help. But all of a sudden, they've come back."

"Well, let's go to his room and look after him."

He caressed her cheek with his thumb. "No, love, you just

go back to sleep."

"What?"

"Go back to sleep."

"Uncle Jordan?" Jim moaned from down the hall.

"You expect me to just go back to sleep while he's suffering? Take me to his room."

"You don't need to worry yourself."

"Too late." She'd been brushed aside before. Not now. Not when Jim was in pain. She didn't know exactly what she could do for Jim, but she was *not* going to be brushed aside again.

"Kayla—"

Lacing her arms around his neck, she held a death grip on him. "You're not leaving unless you take me."

Kayla guessed Jordan would have argued some more, but Jim cried out again. He carried her down the hall and placed her in the chair next to Jim's bed.

Pain contorted Jim's face, his eyes squinted shut. The bedspread and sheets were thrown to the end of the bed. His legs moved slightly, as if a mild vibrator was inside them.

"Shit," Jim moaned. He opened his eyes as Jordan sat beside him. His gaze shifted from his uncle to Kayla. Pain mingled with surprise. "What are you doing here?" he asked of Kayla.

"Just wanted to help, if I could."

"Well, you can't! Get her out of here."

Jordan took the wet washcloth that was on the bedside table and brushed it on his nephew's forehead. "She just wants to help."

"Fuck her! Isn't it time for the medication yet?"

Jordan cringed. He was used to Jim's foulness, but Kayla wasn't. He didn't want her to be exposed to it. He glanced her way. "Perhaps I should take you back?"

She shook her head.

"Hello! Am I even in the room? Medication?" Jim bellowed.

"Jim, you know it's not time yet. And you're being very rude."

"Fuck it! Fuck her!"

"Perhaps it would be best if you tried some visualization techniques, Jim."

Caught between scolding Jim and talking Kayla into going back to his room, Jordan simply stared at her. How was she staying so calm?

"Fuck visualization!"

"Colorful vocabulary. Ever thought of broadening it?"

Another tremor silenced Jim for a minute. But only a minute. "Shit."

"Well, at least it's new."

Jordan sat back and watched the two. Jim with his foul mouth. Kayla with her stern one.

"Visualization. You know, pretend you're someplace else. It may ease the pain slightly."

"Stupid shit," Jim mumbled.

Apparently ignoring him, she continued. "When I wanted to get away from the pain during rehab, I did visualization. The therapists all told me to think of a beach or something. Forget that." She winked at Jordan and then looked back at Jim. "That was silly. So I visualized Luke Skywalker instead."

Jim snorted. "Luke Skywalker? How stupid!"

"Hey, pal, Luke Skywalker was nothing to scoff at. He was *gorgeous* and he saved the planet. His family was a bit dysfunctional, but I wasn't picky."

Jordan glanced over to see Jim with his eyes open and his interest peaked. Jordan could still see Jim's tremors, but they were slower now. The tears on his face were drying.

"And what did you and Luke do?"

"Young man, a lady never tells all."

"Well, I've never done this before. Help me out."

"Hmm." Kayla glanced around the room. Jordan followed her gaze as it fell upon a poster of Rachel Hunter barely clad in a flimsy excuse for a bathing suit. "Something tells me you like Rachel Hunter."

Jim smiled and glanced at the poster, too. "Maybe."

"Well, to start you off, I would simply say imagine Rachel on the beach in that swimsuit and you're there, too."

Jim closed his eyes. And smiled. "Uh-huh."

The concern Jordan had that Kayla couldn't handle Jim's alter ego melted into admiration. Damn, she was good.

"The sun is warm, the sky is crystal blue."

"Yeah, yeah."

"Now please tell me you don't need my assistance beyond that."

"No help needed." Each word was stated as Jim's head nestled further down into the pillow. Only a few minutes passed and then the deep, even breaths expelled from Jim's lips.

Jordan pulled the covers up and over him, turned out the light, and carried Kayla back to his bedroom.

They both climbed under the covers, but he wouldn't let her turn out the light yet.

"You're amazing. Where did you learn that?"

"Some of my clients have told me about it. And I was told to try it myself when I first woke up in the hospital." Her gaze turned serious. "Don't ever brush me aside again, Jordan. Don't try to protect me. I'm a grown woman."

Her eyes widened. She seemed to be saying it for not only his benefit, but her own.

"All right."

He unbuttoned the shirt she wore. "So, it was Luke Skywalker that lit your fire, huh?"

She laughed. It made him feel safe, peaceful. In the past, during Jim's attacks, he had an empty bed to return to. The worry and the fear would fester because there was nothing to distract him. Until now.

"Guess my secret's out."

He pulled the shirt from her shoulders. He took a small nip of one. "And what exactly did this visualization involve?"

He moved from one shoulder to the other, nipped again.

"As I said before," she said on a moan as his tongue dipped into her ear, "a lady never reveals her secrets."

"Well, what do I have to do to get you to tell me?"

His hands glided to cup her breasts.

"Oh, I'm sure I can think of something."

Kayla spent Christmas Eve and Christmas day at Jordan's.

She even brought Sammy along, allowing him to join in the festivities. For Jim she'd bought a journal. She purchased a black sweater for Jordan, a purely selfish deed. He looked so ruggedly handsome in dark sweaters that her mouth watered just to look at him in one.

She received some sweet smelling perfume from Jim. Profoundly touched by it, Kayla wore it everyday. Her gift from Jordan was a set of gardening tools and gloves. He promised to teach her how to use them once spring returned to the town of Duncan.

On New Year's Eve, Jordan invited Maggie, Jake, some of Jim's friends, and Kayla to a party at his house. A year ago, she and Sammy spent an uneventful evening watching the ball descend in New York's Times Square on television.

Looking out the front window, Kayla was pulled back from remembering her lonely past by a warm hand on her shoulder. She looked up to see Jordan smiling.

He pulled up a chair next to her, and said, "You were off somewhere. Where were you?"

"In the past. But I'm back now."

She gently caressed his face, a gesture that had increased in quantity lately. "It's a lovely party. It was nice of you to invite Maggie and Jake."

At the mention of those two, they looked behind them to see Maggie and Jake in the corner of the living room. Maggie sat on Jake's lap as she whispered something into his ear that made him chuckle.

"I'm so happy for her," Kayla said with a sigh. "She deserves to be happy."

"You deserve to be happy, too."

And with all sincerity and honesty, she responded, "I am, Jordan. I truly am."

He smiled and kissed her slowly, deeply. Desire began to swirl in her belly.

"Ten, nine, eight..." the crowd began to count.

Jordan pulled away and winked. "We'll finish this next year."

"Jordan is so cool to let us stay here."

Kayla turned to her best friend. "Yeah. He and I were worried about anyone driving tonight. Too many idiotic drivers on the road."

"Listen to you." Maggie smiled.

"What?"

"*He and I.* You two are such a couple. It's great."

Kayla transferred a stack of towels from her lap to the bed next to where Maggie was sitting. "Yeah, I guess we are." *We are*, she mused. It was a delicious thought.

"New year, new beginnings," Maggie mused out loud. She spread her arms out and plopped back on the bed. "This is going to be an awesome year, I can feel it."

"Of course it is, bride-to-be."

Maggie leaned up on her elbows. "I'm not the only one, dear sis."

"Do I dare to interrupt a female bonding moment?"

Both ladies turned to see Jake in the doorway. Jake's straight, dark hair barely skimmed the top of the doorway as he entered.

"I suppose so," commented Kayla. "Do you two have everything you need?"

Kayla glanced back and forth several times from Maggie to Jake, but there was no response. She could've been invisible for all they knew. Maggie and Jake only had eyes for each other.

"Right," murmured Kayla. "Well, I think I'll say good night now."

Upon leaving the room, she smiled when she heard the bed strain under the extra weight and the sound of Maggie's sigh. Kayla knew exactly how she felt.

Kayla found Jordan in the living room dumping paper plates and cups into a wastebasket.

"Everyone settled in?" he asked.

"Seems to be. Are Steve and Keith in Jim's room?"

"Yeah." Jordan saw the look of concern skim across her face. "He'll be fine, Kay. The boys know about the leg tremors. I discussed it with them and their fine with it. Besides, we're right down the hall if they need us. Relax."

He relaxed a bit himself by verbally acknowledging Jim would be okay. Tonight was the first sleep over Jim had had since before he was diagnosed more than eighteen months ago. He was worried, but knew the sleep over would do Jim more good than anything his uncle could provide.

"Right. Need anymore help?"

Jordan dumped the last bit of trash into the wastebasket. He left it at the end of the couch and came to kneel in front of Kayla. "Yeah, I need help with something."

"What?"

"This." He kissed her. The beat of desire began to drum in his head. Following the beat, he began slow and steady. But as the beat took hold of him, possessed him, he did the same with her mouth. Possessed.

"Jordan..."

"What, love?" He enjoyed the way her breath came out in a rush right after he kissed her.

"When you kiss me like that..."

"Yes?"

"I can't think."

He smiled. "Good. Let's hope you don't think all night."

He followed her down the hall. She parked next to the bed. With upper body strength that still amazed him, she transferred from her wheelchair to his lap. He smiled when she leaned into him.

She'd been so frightened when they first made love. But there was acceptance now in her ease with him. And therefore he wanted to explore her more, teach her more.

She laid back, her hair spilling over the pillows like an angel's halo. The beat swam from his head down to his heart, filling it with a sweet ache. For her.

Since she seemed at ease, he helped her off with her clothes.

The beat raced down to engulf his loins.

Swallowing hard on his desire, he knelt down and flicked his tongue over her breast that was made of satin. Her nipple hardened under his tongue's touch.

The beat was stronger now as he explored more of her skin. It drummed hard in his fingertips, in his ears. But the beat did not drown out her moans.

He returned to her lips, to the heat her mouth offered. "I want to show you more," he whispered.

"More?" Her eyes were closed, but he still felt her tense below him. Ah, so there still was apprehension, he mused.

"I want to please you. Let me show you."

She opened her eyes and smiled. "You already please me."

"Let me show you more."

There was a pause, and Jordan wondered if he'd asked too much.

"Yes, show me."

She really did trust him now, he thought. And he didn't plan to disappoint her.

He kissed her again, then let his tongue mark a moist trail from her chin to her womanhood. He kissed the inside of each calf, drawing nearer to her center. The scent of her made the beat drum three times faster. Then his tongue separated the folds of her womanhood and drew deeper to flick over her most sensitive flesh.

She quivered under his touch. As his tongue kept in rhythm with the beat, she squirmed. His name echoed from her lips as her walls shivered around his tongue.

Her trembles washed over him, into him, mixing with the rapid beat that had overtaken his entire body.

Her trembles continued as he returned to her mouth.

"Wow," was all she could utter between rapid breaths.

"Did you like that?" he asked.

With one raised eyebrow, she asked, "Was my scream of satisfaction not loud enough?"

He laughed. "Yeah, it was loud enough. Think you busted my eardrums."

She playfully punched him. "Well, it's your own fault, you animal."

The beat of her heart beneath his hand had his own pulse doubling again. But he was unsure about attempting anything else tonight. She'd stiffened at his suggestion at first. Perhaps she wasn't ready. The beat still possessed his body, evoking images of what he'd like to do to her. But…

"Jordan?"

"Yes, love?"

She smiled as she brushed her fingertips over his cheek, her thumb along his bottom lip. "Would you show me some more?"

"Gladly."

Chapter Twelve

"Happy first of February, folks. Mother Nature has decided to celebrate this day by dropping eighteen inches of snow on the area. State and county government offices are closed today. As for school closings, here's the long list."

Kayla rolled over and turned off the radio. Hmm. No work today. And she was stuck at Jordan's house. What wonderful things could they do to pass the time?

Thoughts, images, formed and faded in her mind. All sexual. She was becoming brazen. Jordan had turned her into a lustful woman. She closed her eyes and said a prayer of thanks for that.

"I think you're stuck here for the day," Jordan said as he entered the room.

"I just heard on the radio. Where's Jim?"

"I just found him at the computer. He and Steve are having an internet chat about their project."

"Well, what are we to do with ourselves then?" she asked, trying to look serious.

"Hmm. Well, remember how I promised to show you…more?"

"Yeah."

"Well, perhaps it's time we changed venues?"

"Huh?"

"I'd like to give you a bath."

Soapy water lathering over his body. His wet hands drawing circles over her skin. Two slippery bodies sliding into one another.

Lust pulsed a heafty beat inside her body at the mental image. But she sighed heavy and shrugged her shoulders. "Well, if you can't think up anything better to do, I guess we could."

With a smug smile on both their faces an hour later, they ventured into the hall.

"I'll go fix brunch if you go check on Jim," Jordan said.

"Deal," she replied.

Kayla found Jim at the computer, punching away on the keyboard. "May I interrupt?"

Jim looked up. Kayla sure was a pretty woman. But it was more than that. She was cool, too. She'd helped him find this writer's group that he'd been in for a few months now. And although it had bugged the hell out of him at first, he was grateful for the comfort she offered during his leg tremors. But the coolest thing about Kayla was that she lit up his uncle's life. "Yeah, sure."

Kayla wheeled to the computer. "Jordan's in making brunch. Hungry?"

"Starved, but I munched on stuff before I hit the computer."

"We shouldn't have overslept like we did."

Overslept, my butt, Jim thought. He wasn't a kid anymore. He knew exactly why they were late in getting up. And he thought that was pretty cool, too.

Jim saved his work and shut down the computer. He pulled back his chair to leave, but stopped as he was about to pass Kayla. "Listen, Kayla, about the other night."

"No, Jim, not again."

"But I want to apologize—"

"You try to apologize every time and every time I tell you not to."

"But I feel so bad when you hang out with me during a bad episode and I cuss at you."

"It's okay, Jim."

"But—"

"Jim." She placed her hand on his arm and gave a gentle squeeze. "I understand. Maybe not the exact pain, but I understand the frustration, the feeling that you have no control. The cussing even helps a little. I know."

"You know?"

"Sure. During rehab, I cussed like a sailor."

It was a striking image, Kayla cussing a blue streak. "Really?"

"You bet. It helped get some of the anger out. Freaked my parents out." She laughed. "It's funny now, remembering the look on my parents' faces."

Jim laughed, too. "I can imagine."

Her laughing ceased and she patted his arm before she withdrew. "So you see, Jim, it's okay."

Yeah, she was pretty damn cool. "Okay."

"No more apologies. Agreed?"

"Agreed. I'll go see if I can help Uncle Jordan."

Kayla watched him leave the room. He was such a bright boy. No, he wasn't a boy anymore. He was nineteen and a man now. A very bright man, she thought.

She used the phone to check her voicemail at work. But then she lingered awhile in the den.

A large mahogany desk was flanked between the two windows that faced the side yard. In each corner stood a tall bookshelf, cluttered with books on gardening and flowers. Kayla's gaze traveled to the right of the den's entrance, where a deep red sofa complimented the dark wood of the room.

On close inspection of a bookcase, her gaze fell upon a shelf that contained some of Jordan's yearbooks. Thinking it would be fun to see what he looked like when he was younger, she crossed the room and picked up his college yearbook. She flipped through the pages, finding Jordan in the "M" section. She laughed at the thick hair and mischievous gaze that stared back at her. Smiling, she continued to flip through the book, randomly reading some of his friends' notes of congratulations and best wishes. And that's where she found it.

Jordan,

We've had some wonderful times and some awful ones. I'm sorry that things had to turn out the way they did. Perhaps, in time, we will realize it was for the best. I do wish you all the happiness in the world.

Love,
Penny

So, her name was Penny. Kayla's feminine instincts told her that Penny was somehow involved in whatever had happened to Jordan in college. She wasn't sure whether to ask Jordan about Penny or not. Was this something he wanted, needed to talk about? Did she want to hear about his previous love?

"Hey, darling, breakfast is ready."

She looked up to see Jordan in the doorway.

The face that had been lit with passion only an hour ago now dimmed as she looked at him. His insides began to twist. "Kayla?"

"Who was Penny?"

Penny. The name could inflict more of a blow than a fist could. He'd put her, the whole incident, behind him. But now Kayla looked at him with expectancy. How would he explain? "I haven't heard that name in years."

"I'm sorry, Jordan. It's none of my business. I didn't mean to pry." She closed the book with more force than he thought was necessary. She returned his yearbook to the shelf and moved towards him. He blocked her exit with a hand on her shoulder. She stiffened.

"Kay, I—"

"If you don't want to talk about her, it's okay."

"No, no I want…need to tell you. But, breakfast is ready and Jim's hungry." He paused, until she had no choice but to look up at him. "We *will* discuss this after breakfast."

Silence was an uninvited visitor to the meal. Not one word was spoken as scrambled eggs and bacon were nibbled. Jim must have picked up on Jordan's and Kayla's raw nerves because he excused himself from the table after gulping down his food. She and Jordan cleared off the table without a word to each other.

After, they returned to the den. Jordan sat on the sofa in front of her and prayed for guidance.

"It happened eleven years ago, when I was twenty-four and still thought that I was immortal," he began without preamble. The memories flickered to life as he spoke. "I met Penny Simmons in my business management class. She was very attractive. Blonde, curly hair, great figure. She wasn't very bright, but her looks caught everyone's attention. All the guys were after her, including me. I was used to getting the girl then." Back then, it had always taken very little for him to get the girl he wanted. "I was lucky to get her as my partner for the class project. Penny and I were attracted to each, so we started sleeping together."

His finger lifted Kayla's chin, which had lowered. "You weren't the first, Kay. There were others before you." He knew the words must have stung her. For the first time in his life, he regretted it.

"I figured there were. But hearing about it is a lot different than just knowing about it."

"Since you asked, I have to tell you all of it."

She sighed. "Okay."

He took a deep breath and let it out slowly. "Around finals, Penny found out she was pregnant. I was so scared when she told me. I was still young, carefree. That kind of responsibility terrified me. I had no idea how much joy there could be. I only learned that later from watching Thomas with Jim.

"Anyway, I couldn't think straight once Penny told me. She couldn't either. After some of the shock wore off, we sat down and did our best to discuss our options. Marriage was just as scary as the baby. I didn't even know how I felt about abortion. She could have the baby and I could do my best to support them. All the choices were so overwhelming.

"After agreeing, I thought, to wait until after finals before any decisions were made, we didn't see each other for a week. When I did see her again, she told me she'd been too distraught to handle it anymore. She'd had an abortion."

The shock and the guilt washed over him again like a wave upon the sand.

"After the abortion," he continued, "we never spoke again. When I returned home, I told no one. I put it out of my mind for many years. But when Thomas and Beverly moved back to town, I became close to Jim. I saw how much Thomas loved his son, and I began to remember what had happened between Penny and me. I began to think of what it would've been like to be a father to that child that was never born. I fell in love with Jim, and vowed to myself that if I couldn't be a father, I'd be a damn good uncle. That's why I stayed around when a small part of me wanted to be adventurous like my brother. I stayed to help when Mom and Pop got sick and died. And now I'm taking care of Jim. It helps me to think that by helping Jim, I'm making up for what I lost so many years ago."

He ended then, his hopes and fears verbalized for the first time. For a moment, it felt damn good to tell someone. But then his gaze landed on Kayla. Her gaze was stoic.

"I'm not sure what to say, Jordan. You should've told me. Remember I asked you to not keep anything from me. I don't like that. I don't like being coddled and protected like a child."

She had a point. "You're right. I was afraid this would scare you off."

"You shouldn't have lied."

Anger and disappointment laced her words. And struck him deeply. He leaned forward and grasped her hands. He felt a shimmer of relief when she didn't pull away. "This doesn't take away my feelings for you. What happened, happened. Don't let this change your feelings for me. I'm still the same man who loves you." He still saw indecision written all over her face. "Are you going to run away from me now?" He found himself gripping her hands for fear she would leave.

"I'm not going to run away. You didn't run when I told you of my past. I'm still in a little bit of shock though. I'll need a little time. But," she said as she took her turn at lifting his chin with her finger, "I still love you."

Relief drowned out the guilt and pain. He let go of her hands only to grip her shoulders and bring her towards him. His lips were tentative, knowing she still was angry with him. Her lips offered nothing but forgiveness and salvation.

They pulled away to gulp air. "Never keep anything from me, understand?" Kayla asked. "It reminds me of when I was young and people were afraid I'd break because I was weak. Back then, I let them because I didn't know any other way to handle it. But not now, Jordan."

"Not now; not ever."

"Now, we better go find Jim. He raced out of the kitchen after breakfast. I think he picked up on our bad vibes. We better go tell him it's safe to come out of his room now."

Chapter Thirteen

With every turn of the dirt, the ground became darker. Kayla pulled out another weed and added it to the pile next to her. She picked up the shovel Jordan had given her for Christmas and dug deeper to make sure she'd gotten every last strand and leaf.

"How's it going?"

Kayla squinted against the bright March sun to look up at Jordan. "Not bad."

Jordan kneeled next to her. "Yeah, not bad at all. Now that you learned what is and isn't a weed."

"Smart ass. Just because you know doesn't mean the world knows, Mr. Michaels."

He laughed. "You're turning into a quick learner, Ms. Jennings. Ready for a break? I got iced tea in the fridge."

"You bet."

Once inside, they took turns washing their hands and arms.

Sitting at the kitchen table, they gulped down the cool tea.

"Kay, you haven't said a word about Penny since the day of the storm."

It was true. She had yet to decide if she wanted to. "No, I guess I haven't."

"You must have some sort of reaction."

"I think, in the end, it worked out. Penny and you were not at a stage where you could've handled a child. You were strangers to each other. And I can see why you have regrets."

Knowing it was an important question, she paused then asked, "Do you want to have children, Jordan?"

"Yes. Not to replace the child I could've had. That child's gone. But children would bring a certain kind of happiness to my life that only children could bring. Do you?"

"I don't know. I never thought it would be an option. I

didn't think it was a possibility. Now, things are different, thanks to you, Mr. Jordan Michaels." She grinned. "Very different."

She sobered as she verbalized a life long fear. "I don't know if I can have children, Jordan. I've never really discussed it with myself, let alone a doctor."

"Well, we know now that you're capable of many things." He smiled, winked. "Perhaps you can do even more."

He had showed her what she was capable of. Now it seemed her possibilities were endless.

She moved around the table so that they were face to face. "Do you know how very amazing you are?"

He grinned and a slight blush crept to his cheeks. She'd embarrassed him a bit with her compliment, she mused. How could this strong, passionate man blush at a simple compliment?

She leaned forward, kissing him deeply, enjoying the moan that escaped his lips.

They would have continued, if it had not been for the phone ringing. Jordan reluctantly pulled away and answered it.

"Hello? Oh, hi Steve. What?" Kayla heard wrenching fear creep into his voice. "Is he okay? Where did they take him? We'll be right over."

Turning slowly back towards Kayla, he hung up the phone. The blush she'd just seen on his face paled and he gripped the telephone with white knuckles. "Jim had another relapse. He was over at Steve's, working on their book, when he began to have trouble with his legs. Tremors again. Steve said he was in so much pain that he called an ambulance because he didn't know what else to do. They took him to Duncan General Hospital."

Oh, God, not Jim!

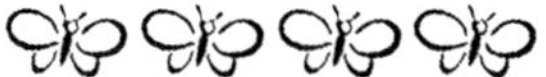

Despite his anxiety, Jordan patiently took the time to help her out of the van and into her wheelchair. At the hospital's information desk, the receptionist informed them that Jim was still in the emergency room.

At the nurse's station, Jordan quickly explained who he was and asked of Jim's whereabouts. While waiting for the doctor,

Kayla saw Jordan's face pale as each moment ticked by. She slid her hand into his and gave a gentle squeeze, a silent signal of moral support.

"Mr. Michaels?"

Jordan turned around. Kayla pushed her chair back to face the man.

"Yes?" replied Jordan.

"I'm Dr. Rhinor. I've been attending to Jim since he came in. He—"

"How is he?"

"Better. We gave him Dantrium. It's a medication to reduce the leg tremors. He seems to be responding well to it. But I want to keep him overnight for observation."

"Can we see him?" Kayla asked.

"Sure, but just briefly. He's exhausted. Please follow me."

They entered a room with beds lining each wall. Patients filled just about every one. Dr. Rhinor walked to the middle of the room, approached a bed that was cocooned by a faded yellow curtain, and opened it. "I'll go check on a room for him. I'll be back in a moment."

Jordan walked up to the head of the bed and looked down at Jim. She knew he was holding his fear at bay for his nephew's sake.

Jim's skin looked like it had been dipped in paste, his breathing deep and rhythmic. An IV pricked his left hand, and dried blood crusted around the entrance to his skin. His ashen complexion blended with the white sheet that enfolded him. He looked like a mummy. From the cubicle next to them, she heard soft crying and a female physician murmuring condolences. She pushed her chair to the head of the bed and held Jim's lifeless hand. Jordan pulled up a chair and held his nephew's other hand.

After about twenty minutes of silence, Jim began to stir. His eyes opened and they landed on Jordan.

Jordan said, "Hi."

Groggily, Jim replied, "Hi."

He turned his head and looked up at Kayla. "Hi, Kay."

Softly, she said, "Hey, Jim, how ya feeling?"

"Very tired, a little dizzy." He paused. "I'm sorry about

this. I didn't mean to interrupt your weekend."

Within Jim's solemn gaze, she saw a weariness and embarrassment that she recognized and understood. Kayla could tell Jordan was about to say something, but she beat him to it. "No, sir, you are *not* apologizing for anything, do you understand me?"

Jim sheepishly grinned, and said, "Yes, ma'am."

With calmness Kayla knew he didn't feel, Jordan said, "She's right, kid. No apology needed."

Their heads turned when the doctor entered.

"Hello, Jim. Have you been under a lot of strain lately, done a little more than you should've, son?"

"Well, I've been working on that book lately. And I've been working on stuff with this new writing group. My friend and I've been stayin' up late some nights."

"It's just a theory. We can't say for sure what will cause an exacerbation, or acceleration, of MS. But, I think you need to rest more, eat a little bit better. For now, we're going to keep you overnight for observation. We'll move you to the fourth floor."

As the orderlies and nurses prepared Jim and took him up to the fourth floor, Jordan and Kayla followed close behind. Once Jim settled into his room, the medication took over, and he fell asleep. Jordan and Kayla sat quietly, letting the drama of the day catch up to them. Jim was going to be all right now.

Eventually, Jordan offered to call someone to take Kayla home.

"Oh, no, I'm not budging. I'm staying right here."

Jordan gave her a tired grin and didn't offer again.

Instead, she pulled herself out of her wheelchair and into his lap. She'd seen the naked fear in Jordan's eyes when Steve called. And although the doctor had reassured them that Jim would be all right, she still saw shadows of anxiety swimming in Jordan's tired eyes. She wanted badly to hold him, to give him some of her strength.

They held each other, exchanging silent comfort throughout the night.

Chapter Fourteen

Sliced turkey squished between two slices of American cheese, coleslaw, red delicious apples hand picked from nearby orchards, pink lemonade that tickled the tongue, and chewy, melt-in-your-mouth chocolate chip cookies.

Mixed aromas from the enticing food caused Kayla's mouth to water and her stomach to grumble.

"Hungry?" Jordan asked.

"Mmm," was her only reply as she dove into her sandwich.

She sat on Jordan's plaid blanket in his backyard. The flowers in the garden bloomed with vivid colors and tantalizing scents. Tulip buds were open, revealing the secrets they'd kept tightly concealed all winter. The scent of freshly mowed grass, mixed with honeysuckle, drifted along the spring breeze.

Kayla glanced up at Jim's window. He'd slowly recovered from his visit to the hospital, but he was still weak. She thought it commendable that he insisted on continuing his book with Steve. Jim's friend came over to the house several times a week, although his stays were shorter than usual.

With the windows open to let the spring air in, Jordan and Kayla could hear Steve and Jim's laughter.

"It's so good to hear him laugh," Jordan said before he took a bite out of his apple.

"Yes, I agree." She heard them laugh again and her heart beamed.

Placing the apple on the blanket, he wiped his hands and face with a crumpled napkin. "You've been wonderful, Kay. You've spent countless nights talking to him, supporting him and his book. You've stayed home from work to care for him a few times when I had to go to the nursery. And, most especially, you've been there for me."

She smiled. "I wanted to do all those things, Jordan. I love Jim. He's a part of your family, a part of who you are. And I also like him as an individual. I was glad I could help. It made me feel as if I was part of a real family."

"At the end of this month, it'll be a year since we met."

"Amazing, isn't it?"

Jordan bent to kiss her. It wasn't rushed. Rather, the kiss was slow, filled with restrained passion and undeniable love.

When he pulled away, he said, "I've been thinking about something for a long time. I thought of putting it off, but this feels like the right time."

With the unrestrained laughter of Jim and Steve echoing from the house, he knelt in front of her, gently grasping her hands. Puzzled, she watched his hands as they wrapped around her own like a cocoon.

Jordan looked at her with that grin that melted her heart, and said, "I love you. You've supported Jim and me through a lot. I've enjoyed your company, our conversations, and our lovemaking."

She grinned at his last remark.

"I can't imagine my life without you now. Will you marry me, Kayla?"

Her jaw dropped. After all the miracles that had taken place in the last year, she hadn't expected another one.

"Kay?"

"I'm sorry, Jordan, you just caught me by surprise."

"Is it really such a surprise to you that I would want to marry you?"

"This whole year has taken me by surprise. Meeting you, falling in love with you, the things you've taught me. I didn't think any of this was possible."

"Now you know it is. And there are so many more possibilities for us in the future, if you'll be my wife."

When she realized that her stomach was doing somersaults of happiness rather than uncertainty, she allowed her heart, once again, to answer. "I love you, too. Yes, I'll marry you."

Peace. It flowed over him, through him, like a gentle summer breeze. He clasped her shoulders and laughed as they tumbled together onto the blanket.

"So, did she say yes?" Jim yelled.

Their playful tumble ended.

"You asked him first?" Kayla inquired.

He had to, just to be sure. Jim's eyes lit up when Jordan asked how he felt about making Kayla a part of their family. But Jim had kept a bland expression on his face as he mumbled something about it being damn time.

"I asked and he approved." He glanced up at Jim's window. "She said yes."

They heard Jim howl with glee, and it made them laugh in return.

"I think he's happy," Jordan remarked.

"It sounds that way," she said with a grin.

His gaze returned to her. He had to say it because this was right and real. An ordinary guy had found an extraordinary love. "I love you, Kay," Jordan said seriously. "With all that I am I swear that I love you and will do my best to be a good husband."

"I know, Jordan. I know."

Fits of laughter erupted from Jim's bedroom window as she and Jordan kissed again.

Chapter Fifteen

"Look at that hairdo on you, Uncle Jordan!" Jim said with a cackle as he flipped to a page containing a photograph of the Michaels family.

After having spent the afternoon making wedding plans with Maggie, Kayla now discussed them with Jim and Jordan. Talk of weddings had prompted Jim to unearth his parents' wedding album.

Kayla leaned over Jim's shoulder and scrutinized the photo. The long sideburns and fuzzy, finger-in-light-socket hair that adorned Jordan's head was laughable. She looked up at Jordan with a smile. "It's a good thing you aren't going to look that way at our wedding."

"Ha-ha," said Jordan, trying to look deflated, but letting a grin begin at the tips of his mouth. "That was twenty years ago, my dear. Fashion was different. Back then, I was the epitome of cool."

Jim and Kayla exchanged a look and broke into undisciplined laughter. Jordan opened his mouth to protest again, when the doorbell rang.

"Who could that be?" Kayla asked.

"I don't know. I'll go check, as long as you and Jim promise not to make anymore cracks about my hairdo," Jordan said as he got up from the couch.

"We promise," said Jim, as he tried to suppress a giggle.

Jordan laughed. "Oh, I give up." He threw his hands up then left to answer the doorbell, which had rung another time.

Jim continued to flip through the pages of the album, looks of amusement and longing skipping over his face. Although Kayla's eyes were on the album, her ears were attuned to what Jordan was doing. From a distance, she could hear Jordan opening the front door. There was a pause, and then a tentative hello, said in a low, feminine voice. Since it was so soft and timid, Kayla was unable to hear most of the woman's side of the conversation. After an extended pause, she heard Jordan invite the woman in. They approached the living room, but Kayla kept her eyes on the wedding album. As she sensed them enter the room, she lifted her face, with a smile on it, expecting it to be someone from the nursery or one of Jim's friends. Kayla felt her smile freeze in place, however, as she recognized the woman, although she was older now, with shorter hair and a leaner face.

Jordan said, stiffly, "Jim, Kay, this is Penny Simmons, an old friend from college."

Kayla recognized her instantly. Jordan was making the formal introductions for Jim's benefit.

"Penny, this is my nephew Jim. And Kay is my fiancée."

Kayla wanted to hate Penny. Penny had been a part of Jordan's past. An important part, yes, but not a part of the present. But when Penny shook Jim's hand and then Kayla's, she couldn't hate her. Penny's benign amber eyes seemed to be calm and harmless, as if time had matured the naive girl of Jordan's past. Kayla recognized that. It made Penny less of a threat and more like a human being in Kayla's mind.

After Penny shook Kayla's hand, she commented, "Congratulations. When's the wedding?"

"December tenth."

Penny smiled, then looked at Jordan and said, "I'm sorry, I should've called first." After a strained pause, she continued, "Is there somewhere we could talk. Please?"

Jordan and Kayla exchanged a glance. Jim excused himself. Watching Jim's retreating back, Kayla felt sorry for him. She knew he always picked up the bad vibes in any situation.

She smiled a little at Jordan, then at Penny. "I'm sure you two have much to catch up on. I think I'll go in the den and work on the guest list."

Kayla began to move off the sofa and into her wheelchair. Jordan stepped forward to help. She was about to move off on her own when Jordan said, "Excuse me for a minute, Penny. I'll take Kay down to the den and show her where the list is. I'll be back in a moment. Please, make yourself comfortable."

Kayla knew exactly where the guest list was, but kept quiet.

They made their way down the hall and into the den. Jordan closed the door and muttered, "I have no idea why she's here or what she wants." He scowled and flexed his hands into fists.

Kayla knew what it was like when the past was left to fester like an old wound: sporadic aches, nagging regrets. Gently, she lifted Jordan's hand and held it firmly, lovingly. "Jordan, you need to talk to her. You need to work out what happened eleven years ago. I'm not saying you have to become best buddies, but talk to her."

His eyes narrowed. He absorbed what she was saying, one of the many reasons she loved him. He listened to her. Really *listened.*

"Just because she's here doesn't mean—"

"Jordan Michaels, what I'm about to say I've never said to another man in my entire life. I trust you."

His expression softened as he lightly kissed her on the mouth, pulled back, grinned, and said, "I love you."

"I know. Now, go and talk to Penny. I'll be here waiting until you're finished."

Jordan took a deep breath and left the room.

It felt as if he was marching towards his own death.

With thoughts of love and weddings in his mind, he'd opened the door to find Penny Simmons, a participant in the biggest regret of his life. Her appearance had smeared his happy images.

What do I say? he wondered. *I was angry that you did what you did, but it's all in the past. So, how about those Redskins?*

No, it wouldn't be that easy. God, he wished it was.

"Sorry I took so long," Jordan commented as he entered the room.

"No problem." Penny picked up and smiled over a picture frame. "How is your brother? I remember how fond you were of him."

"He's dead."

Jordan watched shock and sadness glide over her face. "Oh, I'm sorry."

"Most of my family is gone now. Jim and Kay are my only

family now."

That seemed to make her uncomfortable. "Maybe I should go. I should've called, but—"

"No, please."

She stopped as she crossed the room. "Are you sure?"

"Yes." *No*. He wasn't sure. But he had no choice now. "Please have a seat."

She did, but she sat at one end of the couch with a rim rod back and tightly grasped hands.

Jordan sat at the other end of the couch, feeling the silence like a suffocating cloth around them.

"You now know about me," Jordan finally spoke. "What about you?"

"I finally got my degree in computer science."

He laughed. "Didn't you start out as a fashion design major?"

A tiny smile broke through the stoic profile. "Yes, but it turns out that I'm better with networks and modems than with scissors and pins."

Jordan tried to merge the image of the younger Penny with the modern one. It was a bit difficult.

"No more drinking parties to the wee hours?"

The small smile grew. "No, I gave those up years ago." She finally looked at him. "Remember Jared's party? The one with the twelve kegs of beer that came with the twelve topless dancers?"

"Only part of it. I was too drunk to remember the second part." Boy, how times had changed. It had been about parties and women back then. Now there were no parties and only one woman.

"We had some good times, didn't we Jordan?"

"Yes we did."

Penny's smile crumbled. "I'm sorry, Jordan. Truly sorry."

He wanted to believe her, but the flood of memories was too raw. "Why did you have the abortion without talking to me?" He'd finally asked the question that had been nagging him for more than ten years.

"I was scared. So scared. A baby would ruin my life."

"But there were other options—"

Penny sprung up from the sofa, as if stung by a bee. She

walked to the window and gazed intently on whatever was beyond the window, as if searching for the right words.

"Do you remember what you told me on our first date?"

He winced. "That I was the only man to make all your dreams come true?" God, why did the pick-up line sound so stupid now? Had he really been so egotistical?

Penny continued to look out the window, but she smiled slowly. "Not that. You told me that you were going to travel the world as soon as you got a pesky degree. Said you were just doing it to get your family off your back. But as soon as you got the degree, you were going to travel. London, Paris, Cairo."

"Yeah, I remember."

She turned towards him then, the image of her as a young woman now slowly gliding into the woman before him. "I know you think I made the decision just for myself. But I didn't. I knew you had big plans too."

"You didn't even give me the choice though, did you?"

"No." She walked back to the sofa and sat down. "For all your partying and girlfriends, you were still honorable. You wouldn't hurt anyone intentionally. I knew you would do the honorable thing and try to take care of the baby. I couldn't let you be honorable at your own expense."

"So I should feel gratitude?"

She sighed. "No. I'm simply explaining what was going through my head at the time. I never explained. I was too scared the night you came over and I told you. I was still reeling from it that I couldn't even explain it to myself."

She leaned forward as if to rest her hand on his, but then she seemed to change her mind and placed it between them. "I'm sorry, Jordan. That's all I can think to say."

Too antsy to sit, it was his turn to approach the window. "Why now, Penny? Why come to me now?"

"I was fortunate to find a wonderful man who married me last year. We met at a software engineers conference two years ago. Anyway, I'm now three months pregnant."

Jordan only murmured his acknowledgement.

"This pregnancy brought back vivid memories of the last one. I had to find a way to explain to you, so I could enjoy the now instead of suffer the past."

"Do you want us to be friends now?" The sinister tone in his voice even startled him, but the anger of the past wouldn't let go.

"Hardly. I just wanted you to understand."

Jordan twisted around to face her. The bitterness and sadness almost gagged him. She'd never given him the chance to choose, to be a father, to be—

His gaze landed on the photo of Jim when he was ten. With a wide, carefree smile, Jim grinned at the camera as he held up the first fish he'd ever caught. Actually Jordan had caught it but had let Jim reel it in.

When his gaze finally made it back to Penny, the tight grip the anger had on his throat had loosened. He'd gotten his chance to be a father. To Jim. And as he glanced towards the den, he realized the happiness would continue.

So I could enjoy the now instead of suffer the past.

It was his turn to sigh. "I'm glad you came." He returned to the sofa. "I wish you much happiness in your new life."

For the first time, Penny truly smiled. "Thank you, Jordan."

Now that his pain had subsided, he glanced towards the den again. *How was Kayla?*

"She must be a special woman."

"Hmm?"

Penny rose from the sofa. "You've glanced towards that room several times. She must be one hell of a lady to have you so concerned."

"She is."

Kayla would've lied if she didn't admit to herself that seeing Penny Simmons in Jordan's house didn't make her feel insecure, resentful. Penny had been able to give Jordan a child, but got rid of it. Kayla now had Jordan, but was unsure if she could give him children. Penny's presence reminded her of that strange twist of fate.

But Jordan had given her so many gifts this past year: love, laughter, security, joy. It was her turn to give him her gift of trust.

Working first on the guest list, she made notes of those able to attend. When she finished, for lack of something else to do, she pulled a novel off the shelf she'd read countless times before. Moving from her wheelchair to the small sofa, she eased into a comfortable position. Knowing she couldn't concentrate on a new story line, she drew comfort from reading a familiar one. For a brief time, she lost herself in the pages of someone else's fictional woes.

When she heard the front door open and close, she checked her wristwatch to see that ninety minutes had gone by. A few seconds later, Jordan opened the den door.

He looked tired, drained. Wanting to comfort, Kayla put the book down and held her arms out to him.

He sat down next to her and lifted her onto his lap. She encircled him with her arms and tried her best to soothe him. The ticking of Jordan's desk clock was the only sound to be heard as they embraced. For many moments, they gave and took from each other only silent comfort and reassurance.

Finally, Jordan spoke. "She was sorry we left each other on such a negative note. She's pregnant now, and she was having memories of the child she lost. She thought that by coming to speak to me, she would find some peace."

Kayla worried as she inspected his drawn mouth and slumped shoulders. But she was a bit relieved to see that some color had slipped back into his cheeks.

"We talked about what happened," he continued. "We agreed that it was for the best, but it still haunts us both. She got married a year ago. She now works as a software engineer. Her baby is due in six months."

With profound love in her heart, Kayla confessed, "I'm proud of what you did. I know you may not feel it now, but it was good for you to talk to her."

He blew out a strained breath. "Yeah, I know you're right." Another pause. "What you said before I left the den, about trusting me…"

"Yes?"

"Was that true?"

Thinking of it now, she realized how true it really was. "Yes. I meant it. I never thought I would say those words to any man. But that was before I met you. I love you, Jordan Michaels, *and* I trust you."

He leaned forward and kissed her. His mouths linked with hers and conveyed messages of love and triumph. She greedily accepted. Pressure built as craving spread low in her belly. Finally, they pulled apart, breathless.

"We better go check on Jim," she said.

"All right. But you're spending the night here."

Now with Penny gone, as well as her anxiety, Kayla smiled. "I wouldn't have it any other way."

They found Jim in the kitchen, munching on chips and soda.

Enjoying the freedom to tease, she joked, "Oh, real healthy diet you got there."

With the classical arrogance of a teenager, Jim replied, "Lay off, Aunt Kayla."

She couldn't help but smile from ear to ear despite his cantankerous reply. She was going to be someone's aunt. Another gift Jordan had given her.

"Did that Penny lady leave?" Jim asked.

"Yep," said Jordan.

With a quick glance at his uncle, Jim asked, "Is everything okay?"

Jordan looked down at Kayla, smiled. Winking at her, he replied, "Everything's great."

All three of them finished the evening with a game of cards. Afterwards, Jordan helped Jim to his room, then lovingly took Kayla in his arms and carried her to his room.

They sat on the bed, next to each other. Kayla lazily unbuttoned his shirt, slipped it off, and tenderly kissed his chest, moving without hurry. Pulling back, she leaned in to kiss his mouth, again slowly. She felt heat again, tempered by tenderness this time.

He pulled her shirt up and over her head. Cool air brushed her skin. Then he reached around and unhooked her bra. This time, there was no shyness, as there had been the first time. Only glory in knowing what she would, *could*, share with Jordan. Tingling anticipation sprung from Kayla's stomach outward to each limb. He lifted her up and placed her at the head of the bed. But instead of lying down, she sat up. "I want to touch you, Jordan. Take your clothes off and lay down next to me."

Fires, wild and rich, exploded in his eyes. He smiled a devilish grin of anticipation and need.

He did what she asked. But he wanted her naked as well, so he assisted in undressing her completely. He lay next to her, naked and carefree. She leaned down to kiss him, sliding down to his tanned neck, then his brawny chest. When her mouth reached his nipples, he groaned. She grinned. Immense female pride rushed through her veins when he groaned again as she administered the same treatment to his other nipple.

Her brash desire enticed him. She'd been so shy, uncertain, during their first time together. Now she was taking control. She was finally comfortable with him. And herself.

Her mouth burned a hot trail from his chest to his stomach. As he fought his escalating desire, her hand reached down and encircled his manhood. "Kayla," he moaned, not able to form any other word. Desire beat in his blood as she stroked. But when her mouth replaced her hand, he could no longer handle it.

"Wait," he said as he sat up and guided her down beneath him. He explored her softness with his hands and mouth, uncovering new secrets and inciting old ones. It was a journey he hoped would never end.

She withered beneath him as his hand glided down to stroke her sensitive flesh.

"Jordan." Her voice, soft and yearning, was like a caress.

He entered her swiftly. His desire and love for her multiplied as her heat met his. But he pulled the reins of his desire in and stopped.

The ecstasy and love had been too much for her to keep her eyes open. But now she opened them out of confusion. Jordan looked down upon her with a smile that also reached his eyes. "I love you, Kayla. Now and always. I want to hear it from you."

She trailed her hand from his taut back, to the amazingly soft skin of his shoulder, to his sun tanned neck, and finally to his stubble-covered face, enjoying the purely male composition of his skin. "I love you, Jordan. Now and always."

He kissed her, making it deliriously difficult to breathe, and then began to move within her.

Two bodies and two hearts shuttered in love and satisfaction at the same moment.

Chapter Sixteen

Fifteen Months Later

"Happy Anniversary, darling," Jordan murmured.

Spent from their lovemaking, Kayla laid naked, lovingly curled in Jordan's arms. Sighing, she eyed the shadowy silhouette of their wrapped bodies outlined on the far wall. She didn't know how it was possible. She felt physically drained, yet emotionally full. "Happy anniversary, Jordan."

"You were so beautiful on our wedding day," he commented as experienced hands leisurely stroked her back.

At his remark, she recalled their wedding day a year ago. The ceremony had been a simple one, at Jordan's house. They had rearranged the furniture in the living room for the few who were in attendance. Jim beamed from his position as best man. Maggie, as matron of honor, still glowed from her own wedding. Also present were Jake and a small number of people from the nursery and Kayla's office. In all, there were only about twenty people. No frills, no unfamiliar faces to connect with forgotten names, no outlandish bill for their limited budget. Just a small gathering of friends to witness the beginning of their life together.

Kayla wore a simple white dress, with lace along the modest neckline and hem. Freshly fragrant lilies garnished her dark, upswept hair. Maggie styled her hair making sure delicate tendrils framed and highlighted the bride's face. As an early wedding present, Jim had given her a gold necklace with a single teardrop pearl as its pendant. Kayla stroked it lovingly as she took one last stock of her image in the mirror.

She'd paused before entering the living room where Jordan and their guests awaited. She knew this was a moment to remember and cherish. To her surprise, she wasn't nervous, only peaceful. She'd finally found a family. When the music began, she took a deep breath and entered the living room.

Making it to Jordan's side, she looked up at him and smiled. He smiled in return and pulled up a chair beside her. He'd insisted that as they took their vows, they be at eye level with each other. She agreed.

The ceremony went smoothly. After they'd made their vows, they kissed with a hopeful passion that Kayla thought was an indicator of the great things to come.

Brought back from her musings by Jordan placing the bedspread over them, Kayla said, "You were handsome, as well, my dear husband."

There was a brief pause, while they let memories flood back. Sleep soon beckoned her as she snuggled closer to her husband. Drifting to sleep, she felt satisfied, sated, and sinfully happy.

"Thank you, Mr. Reed. I'll see you and your son next Monday at noon." Kayla hung up the phone and turned to the short stack of mail that was on her desk. About to open the top envelope, her phone rang.

"Good afternoon, this is Kayla Michaels. How may I help you?"

"Have I told you lately that I love you?"

She grinned at Jordan's question. "I think you did last night, but I never get tired of hearing it."

"I love you."

If her love for her husband was electricity, she could light the entire country for a year. "I love you, too. How's work?"

"Steady. 'Tis the season for spending money, which is fine by me."

"Are you keeping Jim busy?"

"He grumbled this morning about helping out here. Didn't want to hang out at this 'boring, old place', as he put it. But he's a handy worker once he sets his mind to it."

"He's not getting overly tired, is he?" She knew it sounded

motherly, but she couldn't help it.

"He's fine, Kay."

"Okay. Are you going to be late tonight?"

"I hope not. It depends on how busy we get in the next few hours. I'll give you a call."

"All right. Love you."

"Love you, too."

She hung up the phone and smiled. Life was good. *Damn* good. She was a wife and aunt now. She had someone to love and he returned the love. No more wishing for what this was like. She lived it everyday. She had love and acceptance for the first time in her life. Life couldn't get any better.

"Did Jordan just call?"

Kayla turned to see Jenny in the doorway. "Yes."

Jenny walked in and put a stack of papers on Kayla's desk. "I could tell. Only he can put that kind of smile on your face."

She chuckled. "Is it that obvious?"

Jenny smiled. "Yes." She pointed to the stack of papers. "There's the Altman file you requested. And on top is some more mail."

"Thanks Jenny."

Jenny left as Kayla flipped through the mail. Still thinking of Jordan, she pulled *Ability* magazine from the bottom of the stack. She flipped through the pages, her mind more on her wedded bliss than on the content of the magazine. Perhaps she should surprise Jordan with that new lingerie she bought last weekend. She hadn't had the courage to try it on for him yet. Oh, but she was feeling good today. Perhaps after Jim went to bed, she'd model it for Jordan. And he would—

She passed the page too quickly, and had to flip back. She wasn't sure if she read it right. Surely her mind had misunderstood. But once she returned to the correct page, she knew her mind hadn't made anything up. She silently read the title over and over again.

New Technology Offers Hope of Walking to Spinal Cord Injury Patients.

It couldn't be. She'd been told all her life this wasn't possible. She scanned the article, but then tossed it onto the desk as if it had bitten her.

Oh, no, she mused. She wasn't going to get her hopes up...again. Even as interest sparked, she told herself it was absurd. The memory of that dream of dancing in a field with the sun stroking her skin wiggled to life again as she shoved the magazine into her bottom desk drawer.

Now, where was she? Oh, yeah. Modeling lingerie for Jordan...

"All set?" Jordan asked Jim as the young man settled into bed.

"Yeah. Could you hand me that book?" Jim gestured towards a textbook on his dresser.

Jordan retrieved it and handed it to Jim. "I'm pleased to see you so interested in this upcoming class. You're already reading the book before school even starts."

"Well, it's my first college class. Even if it's at the community college."

Jordan was proud of his nephew. And he knew Jim had more hope built up for the writing class than a good grade. After a year of just going to the writing group, Jim had grown restless. His body was weak, but not his mind. His creativity needed to be stimulated. And that's when Kayla mentioned taking a writing class at the local community college. Jim hadn't liked the idea at first because it wasn't a *real* college. But she'd convinced him otherwise. Now it looked as if Jim's reluctance had mellowed into eagerness.

"Well, just don't stay up too late," Jordan commented.

"Uncle Jordan, I'm twenty now. Don't treat me like a child."

Jordan sighed. His nephew wasn't a child anymore. Jim depended on him for mobility and other assistance. But Jim no longer needed Jordan as much when Jim was a child. "You're right," Jordan admitted. "Stop growing up so fast."

Jim rolled his eyes.

Jordan left Jim's room and went to the kitchen. As he dried

the dishes, his thoughts drifted from Jim to Kayla.

She'd been awfully quiet tonight. She still chatted at dinner, but her mind seemed to wander after awhile.

He placed the last dish in the cupboard. And smiled. First, he'd ask her what was wrong. Then once they solved the problem, he'd suggest to her that she try on that lingerie she bought last weekend.

Sitting on the bed with wrapping paper spread around her, she debated for a moment, and finally chose the roll of shiny, solid red paper. Cutting off the proper amount, Kayla placed it on her lap and picked up the package of word processing software that she'd bought Jim for Christmas. As she held onto the heavy box, her mind wandered to the event that had happened that morning.

Discovering the article in *Ability* magazine two weeks ago had startled her. She'd read it and dismissed it. But the possibility of the article being true was too good to ignore. It had festered in the back of her mind for days. She'd put off making the phone call, telling herself it was ridiculous and impossible. But within her grew hope, relentless and steadfast, and she'd finally gotten up the nerve that morning to call. And the call had changed everything.

"Kay."

Brought back to reality, Kayla looked up when her husband called her name. Her eyes focused from the dream world she'd been in to the bedroom and Jordan. He stood in the doorway, looking as handsome as ever. A year of marriage hadn't diminished her attraction for him one bit.

"Did Jim go to bed okay?" she asked.

"Yeah. Uh, you've been distant all evening. What's up?" Sitting on the bed next to her, he caressed her arm with warm, soft strokes. "Is something wrong? I'm a little worried."

Kayla smiled, appreciating his attentiveness. "Nothing's wrong, Jordan. I'm fine."

"There's something though, isn't there?"

Sighing, she put the still unwrapped box, along with its intended wrapping paper, beside her on the bed. Turning to Jordan, she placed a quick kiss on his cheek. Spontaneous gestures such as kissing him just because he was there was one of the many rewards of her marriage.

Leaning back against the propped pillows, she said, "Okay. There's something. But it isn't bad. I haven't told you because I wasn't sure it was possible."

Leaning forward, Kayla pulled open the top drawer of the bedside table, took out the magazine, flipped to the marked page, and handed it to Jordan. "I read this article two weeks ago at the office. I thought the story was a bunch of baloney so I put it aside. But it kept nagging at me."

Jordan took the magazine and glanced at the page. "'New technology offers hope of walking to spinal cord injury patients,'" he read. He put the magazine down and looked up at Kayla with a stunned look on his face.

"The gist of the article is that there's a way to electrically stimulate some of the nerve endings, allowing a possibility of enough regeneration to allow someone like me to walk. I put it off for a while, but the thought wouldn't go away. So I called the researcher that's quoted in the article, a Dr. John Holling. He's located in Baltimore, at Johns Hopkins."

"And what did he say?"

"We talked about the technology and the possibility. He said since I was still fairly young and in relatively good shape, I could be a perfect candidate for the procedure."

Jordan said nothing for several moments, although his face grew taut and his brow furrowed. His silence confused Kayla. "Jordan?"

"I wish you had told me sooner. Have you done some research about this? Do you know if this doctor's the best? Are there any side effects to this new procedure?"

Surprised by his lack of enthusiasm, she frowned. Thinking he would, *should*, be pleased, she defended herself. "Dr. Holling admitted that I would need to go through a battery of tests before he could say for sure that I could undergo the procedure. He also said that it's still in the experimental stages, so he couldn't guarantee anything. But, Jordan, I can feel it in my bones. It could work." She put her hands on his, clutching for emphasis. "It could work, Jordan."

"This is sudden, Kay. I'm not sure what to say."

Disappointed and hurt, she drew back her hands. "I thought you would be happy for me. Just think. I could walk again! Think of all we could do."

She thought that he didn't look convinced.

"I want to read this article," he said as he got off the bed and walked to the doorway, still holding the magazine. "I'm going to have some hot tea. I'll be to bed shortly."

Kayla leaned back against the pillows again as he left the room, baffled by his reaction. Dread slowly took seed in her mind, a feeling not unlike the one she'd felt the night Penny visited. But that was ridiculous, she thought. She was simply overreacting. Perhaps he was just surprised by it all. She certainly had been at first. Maybe she needed to give him some time to get adjusted to the idea. Yes, that was it, just more time. Humming *Silent Night,* she began wrapping Jim's gift as her spirits lifted.

Chapter Seventeen

Kayla wasn't sure how much time she should give Jordan, but she was beginning to think a century wouldn't be enough.

She hadn't brought up the magazine article for several weeks. Throughout their holiday celebrations, Jordan had acted like nothing had changed. For a while, she let him. But she thought of the article often. Every time she'd get up the nerve to call Dr. Holling for a consultation, she'd back down. In her head, she knew the procedure was experimental. But her heart refused to relinquish her dream. Dancing had been the fuel of her soul since that enchanting moment when she'd seen Kelly and Caron glide through the streets of Paris. The accident, she'd believed, snuffed out that fuel, that fire. This new possibility was sparking it back to life.

But was she prepared for whatever result she would get from the procedure? Now, after struggling twenty years to form and accept her identity, including her disability, could she go through a procedure that could change all that?

At the end of January, sick and tired of playing the Maybe game, Kayla gave up. Maybe she wasn't a perfect candidate for the procedure. Maybe she was. Maybe, by this time next year, she and Jordan could go on a cruise and swim in the Bahamas. Maybe…

The earliest Dr. Holling could get her in was March first. Numerous hopeful spinal cord injury patients had read the same article she had, eager for the doctor's procedure. Disappointed at the wait, Kayla took a deep breath and summoned her courage to tell Jordan.

The following afternoon she found him in the kitchen, repairing the leaky pipe below the sink. He turned to her when she entered the room and smiled.

"When you're done with that, I need to speak to you," she

said.

"Sure," Jordan replied as he bent to tighten the pipe.

She wheeled herself to the den and waited. Ten minutes later, Jordan strolled in. "Finally got that leaky pipe fixed."

"Good. Thanks. How'd the shipment go last night?" she asked, trying to sound nonchalant while her stomach bubbled with nerves.

Taking a seat on the sofa, Jordan sighed. "Ah, it was a pain. They shipped twice as many shovels as I ordered, but half as many boxes of gloves. I had to unload everything, then called the company this morning to fix the order." He sighed again. "So, what is it that you want to talk about?"

She'd thought it would be best to say it all at once, swiftly, without thought or care for consequences. But now, with much consideration, she tentatively began. "We haven't spoken about this for a month. But I've thought about it everyday. And I got tired of wondering, guessing, hoping. So yesterday I made an appointment to see Dr. Holling on March first."

As she spoke, her eyes focused on a picture frame beyond Jordan's shoulder. But now her gaze returned to his face. Because his countenance was unreadable, she felt fear clutch her stomach. Banking her anxiety, she swallowed hard.

Jordan got up and walked passed her. Although her back was to the desk, she heard him opening and closing several drawers. He soon returned to the sofa with an armful of papers. "I did some research after you told me about the article."

Surprise and anger made a dangerous mix. "Research?"

He stopped flipping through the papers and looked at her with a rarely seen hardness in his eyes. "I was surprised at first. Then angry that you didn't mention it to me earlier. But I calmed after a bit. I gave it some thought, decided to research it. That's what all this is," he said, lifting the pile of papers.

"And what did you find out?"

"I love you, Kayla. I've never demanded or asked anything of you. But I now ask you not to go through with this procedure."

"Why?"

Flipping through the papers again, he pulled out a large, stapled collection of computer generated notes. "The Centers for

Disease Control has done research into Dr. Holling's work. They disagree on its reliability. They also argue there are some side effects that Dr. Holling hasn't made readily available to the public."

"Dr. Holling mentioned some of the side effects, but—"

"There's more. There's been research done on animals, with some positive results, but nothing conclusive on humans. Also—"

"Wait!" Anger sliced deep in her gut and rose to the surface. "Why are you doing this? Why are you trying to take away all my hopes, my dreams?"

He set aside the papers and looked at Kayla with what she thought was hurt in his eyes. "I know you had a dream snatched away from you years ago. That was wrong. You have every right to be upset about it. But you have a life here now with Jim and me."

"Yes, and I'm very happy with my life. This new possibility has nothing to do with whether I'm happy with my life with you."

The only time she'd seen Jordan angry was when she told him of what the Tannen women had said. But with his solemn frown, she wondered if that would change.

"Sometimes we must accept what life has given us."

It sounded like something her mother had said to her when she was a child. She wasn't a child anymore. "Is that what you want me to do? Without even trying?"

"Yes."

"I see." She did indeed, very clearly. "Just like you did."

"Me?"

"Yes." She knew she had a weapon and her anger aimed it. "You gave up your dream of traveling around the world so you could take care of your family. You accepted what life had given you without a fight."

"Hey, wait a minute. This is about you."

"Really? Maybe it's not. You accepted your fate and you expect me to accept mine. But what if you had an opportunity to do what you always wanted to do? What if Jim and I weren't here and you got an opportunity to travel? Would you take it?"

His silence was his answer.

"Then why can't I have this chance, Jordan?"

"You don't know it's safe."

"I think that's only an excuse."

"Why is this so important to you?"

Frustrated, she gripped his arm. "There's so much I could do with the use of my legs. We could go swimming." And dancing, she thought.

"But—"

"I could travel," she continued while creating an image in her mind of each activity, "without having to make accommodations ahead of time for the wheelchair."

"But Jim—"

"And," she grinned at the next image, "we could be more...*creative* when we make love." The smile she gave him flattened when her mind cleared and her gaze fell upon his face. He was angry now. And hurt. "Jordan, I didn't mean—"

"What? That you hate it when I touch you?"

"No, of course not. That's not what I meant. I can't please you like some women could."

"I've never complained because I've never had anything to complain about. But you obviously do."

Oops!

He shot off the sofa. Her hand that had been on his arm was now empty. Anger vibrated off his stiff body and heavy steps. Her heart broke as she watched his retreating steps.

But he stopped as he yanked open the door. He turned around to face her. "I'm afraid. I'm afraid that if you have an unsuccessful procedure, you'll be extremely disappointed. I know you. You've set your hopes so high, darling."

The love that he conveyed in the single *darling* melted her heart.

"But I'm also afraid that the procedure will be a success," he continued. "And you'll come out thinking that you're a better person for having it done. You think you're weak and unworthy now and this procedure will erase all that. If all that was involved were your legs, I'd be happy for you. But your worthiness, your very own identity as a human being, is not wrapped up in your legs. I thought you'd know that by now and not need a procedure to prove it. You may gain the ability to walk, but I'm afraid I'm going to lose you in the process."

The door latched quietly behind him. Kayla felt cool tears slide down her feverish cheeks. Slowly wiping them away, she tried, unsuccessfully, to wipe away the hurt inside as well. With rubbery arms, she pushed the wheelchair to the window behind the desk.

Jordan's angry words played over and over in her mind as she stared out into the yard. Did Jordan have a point? Was her self-identity really based on her ability to walk? Showering without having to maneuver herself into the wheelchair first would be effortless. Planning extra time to get into and out of the van would be unnecessary. Rude stares and whispers behind her back would be a part of the fortunate past.

But what if the procedure didn't work? Would she be content to come home and continue living her life in a wheelchair, as she had been doing for twenty years?

I don't know what to do!

As more tears welled up and overflowed, Kayla realized she had more questions than answers.

Chapter Eighteen

"I said I wanted twenty-five boxes of the twelve inch stakes, not twelve boxes of twenty-five inch stakes," Jordan shouted into the phone. He didn't notice customers stop their browsing to stare at the open door of his office. "Well, I've got the goddamn paperwork right here in my hand and that's not what it says." He plied fingers through his hair and tried to count to ten. He only made it to three. "Look, that's what I ordered. Now if you can't get it right, I'll find someone else to do your fucking job." He slammed the phone down on the receiver, the cord twisted from constantly coiling it about his fingers.

"Problem?"

Jordan looked up from the phone to see Jim in the doorway. "What are you doing here?"

"Nice to see you, too." Jim continued forward until he reached the desk. "Friends of yours?" he nodded towards the phone.

"Just another screwed up order. What are you doing here?" he asked again.

"I was at Todd's studying. His mom needed to run some errands, and since Todd and I were taking a break, we got roped into helping. Just so happened she needed some potting soil."

Jordan clasped his hands in his lap and sat back in his chair. "How's school?" He realized he hadn't asked that in several days.

"I got a C on my last paper and—"

"A C? What's the matter with you, Jim? What happened to your A average?" The anger he felt towards himself and another was aimed at Jim instead.

"But it was a hard paper and I've been sick—"

"That's no excuse! I'm disappointed! I can't believe—"

Jim simply turned and shoved the door so it clapped shut.

He turned back to his uncle. "Bite me."

Jordan's tirade ceased. "Excuse me?"

"I said, 'bite me.'"

"I didn't raise you to speak to me like that."

"You raised me to always use my brain. And I'm going to start using it."

"I—"

Jim placed his hand in the air to stop his uncle. "I've had enough of your childish behavior."

"James Michaels—"

"I'm not going to shut up. I'm an adult now and you're going to listen, even if I have to tape your mouth myself."

Jordan didn't know whether to laugh or yell. He chose silence instead.

Jim took a deep breath. "The pain and anger in the house could be cut with a knife, it's so thick. And I'm sick of being in a house like that."

Jordan sighed. "You're right, you shouldn't be in a house like that—"

"Oh, shut up." It was said with weariness more than anger. "Kayla told me about the procedure."

"Did she?"

"Yeah. And personally, I think you're being selfish."

"Okay, I'll accept your right to speak as an adult. But that last statement goes too far, even for you."

"Perhaps not far enough." Jim leaned on the desk. "You hurt her."

Jordan's heart twisted. He would never want to cause his wife any pain. But then he remembered she inflicted pain, too. *We could be more creative when we make love.* "It's none of your business, Jim."

"She's my family now, too."

Jordan couldn't argue with that.

"When I was first diagnosed, didn't you and dad and mom work hard to find the best doctor in the country?"

How high had that phone bill gotten? Jordan remembered. He also remembered how his family hadn't cared and they'd pulled their resources to pay for the costly phone bill. "Yeah."

"Why?"

Jordan's brow wrinkled. "Why? Because we wanted you to feel better. We wanted you to get well and be happy."

"Isn't that what Aunt Kayla wants?"

This boy—no, man. Jordan had to keep correcting himself. This *man* was surpassing his uncle by leaps and bounds. "This is different." Agitation had him rising and stepping over to his bookshelf to supposedly inspect a shelf of flower books. "Don't you have some homework to do?"

"This isn't like you. You're jumpy, agitated, barking out orders," Jim said, ignoring his uncle's question. "There's something else going on here."

Jordan rolled his eyes, his back still towards Jim. "Are you trying out for a psychology degree all of a sudden?"

There was a pause. Jordan actually thought Jim had fallen asleep. Then there was a sudden snap of the fingers and Jordan turned to his nephew.

"You're scared," Jim said. He smiled as if he'd finally gotten the bonus question correct on Jeopardy.

"Huh?"

"I've seen almost every emotion from you except true anger and true fear. If you were angry, I'd think you'd be silent a lot. You'd probably brood. But I think fear would make you irrational, which fits your profile for the last ten days."

"Jim, this isn't cute anymore." His nephew had hit the hammer on the head. A little too hard. "Go back to Todd and get back to studying."

"But—"

"Jim, this is none of your business! Get the hell out of here!"

Jim's determined mouth flopped down. The triumphant gleam in his eye snuffed out before Jordan could stop his harsh words.

"Yeah. See ya at home." Jim pushed his way to the door and grasped the knob.

"Wait, Jim." Shame swamped him. He'd never spoken to his nephew like that before. "I didn't mean to be so harsh. I'm sorry." He sighed.

Jim spoke without turning to face his uncle. "Don't apologize to me. Apologize to her. Or do whatever it takes. Otherwise we may lose the best thing that's happened to either one of us."

Jim opened the door and left.

Damn kid thought he knew everything, Jordan mentally mumbled. Scared? Maybe for Kayla's safety, but not because he thought he'd lose her. Nah. That would never happen. Because if it did, he'd lose everything. He'd lose the woman who had his heart. A woman who had taught him that after all the losses in his life, he could have something rich and rewarding to look forward to. A woman who elicited a deep desire from him that he'd never imagined was possible. Her hands could be gentle as she soothed Jim's brow or rough and needy as she explored her husband.

He eased back in his chair, stretched. Nah. He wasn't scared. He was terrified.

Jordan was working late at the nursery again. It was an occurrence that had continued since their fight two weeks ago. To avoid another lonely night, Kayla invited Maggie over for dinner. Jake was busy researching and composing a newspaper article. So it was just Kayla, Maggie, and Jim that shared a meal.

Forgetting her woes for a while, Kayla felt relaxed enough to tease. "Boy, Maggie, you sure ate a lot. Isn't Jake a good cook?"

Scraping her plate clean, Maggie devoured the last crumb of her chicken pot pie. Beaming at Kayla, she announced, "I heard it's pretty normal to eat a lot during your third month of pregnancy."

The spoon that was on its way to Kayla's mouth stopped halfway to its destination. "You're pregnant?"

"Yep. A little over three months."

Shock melted easily into pure joy. "Oh, sis, I'm so happy for you!" A pang of envy tugged at Kayla's heart, but she pushed it aside. She allowed only happiness for Maggie to bloom in her heart. Kayla gave Maggie a huge hug. "Is this the same girl who in college said she would never have children?"

Maggie chuckled. "That was before I met Jake."

Kayla leaned back in her chair and beamed along with her best friend. She would become an aunt again. "And what does Jake think?"

"He was surprised when I told him. We weren't exactly planning this, but it's not like we weren't planning it either. It just kind of happened. Now he's ecstatic, although a bit over protective."

"Oh?"

"Well, I've had morning sickness. He insists that I take it easy when he sees me get sick, even though I usually feel better afterwards."

"He means well."

With a grin of appreciation, Maggie admitted, "Yeah, he does."

"Hey, can't a guy get in on the action here?"

Kayla and Maggie turned to see Jim come up along the other side of Maggie. He leaned in and gave Maggie a tentative kiss on the cheek. "Congratulations."

Jim was turning into a gentleman just like his uncle, Kayla thought.

"Why thank you, Jim."

Questions about due dates, baby furniture, and baby clothes swirled amongst the three of them. Kayla noticed how Jim paled when the conversation turned to breastfeeding. He was saved from fumbling over an excuse to leave when the phone rang.

"I'll get it," said Jim, looking immensely relieved. "Hello? Hey, Steve. Okay. Just a minute." Jim muffled the phone with his hand and turned to his aunt. "Aunt Kay, Steve has some free time. I'd like to show him that new software you got me for Christmas. Too late for him to come over?"

"Of course not." Kayla turned back to Maggie and said, "It'll give us a chance to have a real girl chat."

Thirty minutes later after the dishes had been cleared and Steve had arrived, the two women retired to the living room.

"So, have you and Jake thought up names yet?" Enjoying Maggie's good news, Kayla sipped tea, eager for her sister's response.

Maggie sat back on the couch and sighed. "We're just getting to that point. We'll have to move. My little apartment is cozy for two, but it'll be crowded with three."

"God, so much has changed since college," Kayla mused out loud.

"Indeed they have." Maggie's smile flattened and the joy that had been in her voice disappeared. "Have you and Jordan discussed children again?"

Kayla sighed and remembered the countless doctors they'd visited in the last few months. "Not lately. Once we found a doctor who was willing to work with my injury, he said I probably could get pregnant, but he couldn't guarantee it. It's possible for women with spinal cord injuries to conceive and carry a child to term. It just hasn't happened yet for me. Maybe it never will."

"Ah, don't give up yet. Are you and Jordan still fighting?"

Kayla paused to sip more of her tea.

"You're hesitating, so I gather he's still against the procedure, huh?"

"Yeah. He says it's too new to get my hopes up. He seems to think that I'm trying to change myself because I don't like myself, not just because I want to walk."

"Are you?"

Kayla groaned. "Maggie! Not you, too."

"Just listen. And remember I'm your sister of the heart and I love you. Your ability to walk has nothing to do with this. I can see where you would want to walk and dance again. But, Kayla, you've come so far. Remember our long talks in the dorm room about our dreams of being happy, of finding men to share our lives with? We talked of love and happiness, and making a difference in the world. It was a hard fight, but look around." She spread her arms out and up. "We've done it, sis. Don't you see? We found good, loving men to share our lives with. I'm pregnant and you will be; I've no doubt. I have a job I love. And although you may complain about it from time to time, you love your job, too."

She leaned forward and squeezed Kayla's hand. "We've done everything we talked about. It may not have been exactly the way we planned it, but the end results are the same. Do you really need that procedure to prove you're a successful, complete woman?"

Did Maggie have a point? Hearing Maggie's words put a new angle on the situation. Kayla admitted to herself that she was very lucky to have such a good life with Jordan. "I never thought of it that way."

"Look, think it over. If you decide to go through with it, I'll support you. You know that. But do it for the right reasons, Kay."

Kayla heard Jordan come in the front door. When he walked into the living room, she recognized the look of uneasiness on his bedraggled face and in his drooped posture. She'd been seeing that same expression for two weeks, and it was starting to drive her mad.

Maggie looked cautiously from Kayla to Jordan. "Hey, Jordan, late night at the office?"

Jordan's gaze slid from Kayla to Maggie while his mouth broke into only a half-hearted grin. "Yeah, something like that."

"Well, we were having a girl chat, but I'd better get going. See if Jake's home yet."

As Maggie got up, Kayla's gaze shifted from Jordan's empty expression to Maggie's hopeful one. Because she was truly happy for her friend, she said, "You take care of yourself, my dear. Give my best to Jake. I really am happy for you."

Maggie leaned over for a quick hug. Whispering in Kayla's ear, she advised, "Remember, Kay, you've come so far. You don't need to prove anything to anyone."

Maggie turned and gave Jordan a quick hug goodbye, waved at Kayla, and left.

Silence. Kayla hated it, and, as usual, she felt the need to fill it. "Steve's here. Jim wanted to show him the new software."

"Okay. Ready for bed?"

"Yeah."

At this point, he normally carried her to their room. He'd cradle her in his arms; she'd nuzzle his neck. Sighs would be exchanged during their short trip down the hall.

But there was no thrill as she got into her wheelchair and went down the hall alone. No murmured words of love, no nuzzling.

She felt the loss keenly.

In the bedroom, she changed her clothes and got into bed.

Jordan stood in the doorway as if afraid to enter. "I'll go check on Jim."

The weight upon Kayla's heart deepened. She turned off the light, but her ever-growing hopelessness kept her from sleeping.

After what seemed like hours, Jordan returned to the room. The rustle of clothing filled the muted air. She felt the bed give way. Kayla was perfectly still as the bed creaked and the sheets shuffled. Several seconds ticked by as the house settled down for the night. After the commotion of getting ready for bed, the house was suddenly silent.

Kayla couldn't take the deafening quiet any longer. "Jordan?"

"Hmm?"

"With all that I am, I love you. This silence is killing me." Tears sprang to her eyes as she wept into her pillow.

She felt Jordan turn and slip his arms around her. She clung to him as if she was drowning and he was her only life jacket.

"I love you, too, Kayla," he said.

His declaration, whispered right above her ear, released the anger, soothed the hurt.

She turned and wrapped around him as tightly as she could as her tears overflowed. Sobs racked her body as he held her warmly against him. She'd missed this intimacy, this holding of each other. When her voice was controllable and most of her tears had been shed, she spoke. "I need to tell you something."

Pulling away, she focused on his face that was lit by the moon's light. She propped her pillow against the headboard and leaned back, clasping his warm hands in her own. "The night before I met you, I had a dream. I dreamt I was in a beautiful field, warmed by the sun's rays. Fragrant flowers bloomed in rich green grass." She slipped back into that place of unadulterated bliss as she spoke. "I was dancing. I was in a white dress and it twirled at my ankles as I carelessly spun around in endless, gloriously endless circles. It felt so real. So *real*. My legs even tingled when I woke up."

Unhurriedly, she returned from that far off sun-drenched

field. "That was the morning I met you. You walked into my office with Jim, and I couldn't think of anything else but you." She smiled, remembering that moment. Remembering how Jordan's good looks had nearly knocked her out of her chair and how his silky, deep voice sounded like music to her ears. "I often wonder if that dream wasn't predicting us getting together, the wonderful free feeling I have when I'm with you. I love you, Jordan. This procedure has nothing to do with you or my love for you."

Emphasizing her point, she leaned over and kissed him gently on his sweet, solemn lips. "But this is something I have to know for myself. I'm going to see Dr. Holling for preliminary tests. I don't even know if I'm eligible for the procedure. I can't explain it, but I have a need to know, Jordan."

"And what if you can go through with the procedure?"

Unsure, Kayla took in a deep breath and let it out slowly. "I don't know. I haven't thought that far ahead. I've been afraid to hope that far ahead."

"Do you want me to go with you?"

"You should stay here with Jim. I'll ask Maggie to go."

"I'm your husband. I should be with you, Kay."

"Jordan, I know you still don't approve. I can't go and be worried about your reaction. Please, try to understand."

He sighed. "Just don't make any rash decisions without me."

Glad to see the love bloom again in his eyes, she agreed.

His hand brushed her face. "I've missed you."

God, how she'd yearned for his touch. Had it been two weeks? It felt more like an eternity. "I've missed you, too."

She looked so radiant, he thought. A silhouette from the moon made her ebony hair shine as if angel dust had been sprinkled on it. The love in her eyes and in her touch still flabbergasted him. The fear was still there. But then Kayla leaned towards him, into him.

"I never meant to hurt you. I love it when you touch me. Touch me now, Jordan. Touch me everywhere."

Her admission weakened him, enlivened him. His one fear of being inadequate was smothered by her plea. A glimmer of fear lingered. He still didn't approve of the procedure, but all that mattered now was her touch, her voice, her scent. Her.

Her lips played with his until he opened them. He moaned when her tongue met his, when her love reconnected with his. When her thumb trailed along his cheek, he wondered how the hell he'd denied himself the joy of her for so long.

Answering her plea, Jordan made love to her. Sighs and murmurs, caresses and strokes, tenderness and passion.

After, she lay limp and sated next to him. He gripped her body to his, somehow hoping to keep her safe forever. For although he loved her with his very being, he knew he wouldn't be able to protect her from what lie ahead.

Chapter Nineteen

"I appreciate you helping me out, Maggie."

Keeping her eyes on the road, Maggie shook her head. "No problem. It's just one day. Jake's out of town and I'm almost done with my piece on the youth gangs in northern Virginia. One day doesn't hurt."

Kayla turned from her friend to look out the car window. Cars whipped by as Maggie maneuvered up interstate 95, heading towards Baltimore. Dr. Holling's office was located at Johns Hopkins, one of the best hospitals in the country, she knew. His research had been conducted there, including the latest on human subjects.

She took a deep breath, hoping to get rid of the gnawing pain in the pit of her stomach. She'd thrown up that morning, a rarity for her. Her anxiety had tripled overnight, she mused. This was something she wanted, needed to know, she reassured herself. Her mind was convinced of that need, but it seemed the rest of her body wasn't willing to go along.

Turning back to Maggie, she asked, "Why did you agree to help me? I wasn't sure if you would. From the way we spoke last, you were opposed to this."

Maggie shifted lanes smoothly. "I told you I would go along with whatever you decided."

Kayla smiled. Maggie's unquestionable support was a true gift. "You're a good friend. Thanks."

"No problem. Umm, I was wondering…well, you've been quiet since I picked you up. Did you and Jordan have another fight?"

Maggie's question brought back the memory of her conversation with Jordan that morning. Jordan had gotten up with

Kayla. He'd been concerned when she'd gotten sick. He'd tried to talk her out of going, but she felt better afterwards, and didn't want another excuse to delay her. It was now or never, she knew.

Jordan had sat on the edge of the bed, looking like his best friend just died. "Jordan," she'd said, "it's just one day. I'll be back this evening." She'd clasped his hands to soothe his worry.

Jordan turned his hands so they clasped hers and looked up at Kayla. "Then why do I feel like I'm losing you, like I'll never see you again?"

"Please don't make this any harder."

With a kind of sorrow in his eyes that she'd never seen before, he'd said, "Promise you won't make any quick or rash decisions."

"I told you, I'm just going for initial tests. No life altering decisions are going to be made today."

"I love you, walking or not, Kayla."

Her heart had melted. After all this time together, she knew he spoke the truth. She'd learned so much from this man. He simply accepted her. "I love you, too."

Clearing her throat, Maggie brought Kayla back to the present.

"Sorry, Maggie, I guess my mind wandered."

Maggie chuckled. "That's nothing new."

"Ha-ha." Kayla had to laugh. Her best friend knew her too well. "Jordan's still uncomfortable about this procedure. I didn't really give him much of a choice, I guess. I told him I made the appointment then I asked you to take me. I didn't want to hurt him, but he's really against it. I guess there's some research out there that goes against Dr. Holling's work. So Jordan doesn't think I should see him. He doesn't believe the doctor's reliable enough."

"Jordan loves you. He's concerned about you. He's afraid you're going to get hurt."

"I know. But he doesn't realize all the possibilities that we could have if I could walk again."

Instead of making more conversation, Kayla kept quiet, allowing Maggie to concentrate on driving into downtown Baltimore. They made their way down Pratt Street and turned onto Broadway. Kayla barely noticed the people rushing about on their lunch hour or the police officers roaming the streets. Finally reaching the hospital, they parked. Before Maggie got out of the car, she turned to Kayla. "Have you ever thought that maybe it's you who can't see the possibilities you already have?"

As Maggie got out of the car, Kayla felt an uneasiness at her friend's words and tried to brush the feeling aside. Today was a day of new possibilities, she hoped. No more second guessing, no more wondering. With optimism in her heart and irresolution in her mind, Kayla slid into her wheelchair and headed towards her new destiny.

"Shit!"

Jim pounded the keyboard with a closed fist. "Shit!" he repeated.

He stared at the computer screen. Only a sliver of decency stopped him from punching it out. The words were too jumbled in his brain, like static on a radio. He had the thought, pure and perfect. But the path from his brain to his fingertips was short-circuiting. He just couldn't find the right word, the right phrase.

Enough, he thought.

He saved his work and sat back as the computer shut down. The tendons in his hands and wrists moaned from being worked too hard. He should've stopped a few hours ago. But the writing was an excellent distraction. Distraction from worrying about Kayla.

Aunt Kayla now, he thought. He'd like calling her that and knew she did too because she beamed every time he said it. No one would replace his mother. But Kayla had brought with her feminine softness and tenderness that he'd missed. And she was tough, too, he mused. She forced him to keep going when he was discouraged and told him when to slow down when he needed to.

Now he understood a little bit of what his uncle must be feeling. Would she come home and look different? *Be* different?

He envied her. He would never have an opportunity like this. His disease could get worse tomorrow or in fifty years. To be rid of that uncertainty would be a blessing.

But he didn't want his envy to stop her. That's why he wished her well this morning, with all honesty, as she climbed into Maggie's car. But the fear still gave a quiver in his heart. Would she be different?

He rubbed his tense neck. And decided it was time to go check on his uncle.

Jim found his uncle in the living room, his hands wrapped around a wine glass and his eyes glazed over. He debated about leaving his uncle alone. As Uncle Jordan had said, it was none of his business.

He watched Jordan take a heavy swallow of the contents of the glass. No, Jim thought. He'd better keep his uncle company. He was becoming a bit too friendly with that glass.

"Mind sharing?"

Jordan turned to his nephew. His uncle looked as if he was about to say no, but then caught himself. "Sure."

As Jim approached the couch, Jordan got up and retrieved another glass from the cabinet. He poured wine in it and handed it to his nephew.

Okay, his uncle was in deep, Jim mused. Although Jim was twenty, he'd never taken a drink before. Too much medication. But now his uncle had just given him a glass full of wine without a word or lecture. Oh, yeah, his uncle was in deep.

Jim only sipped. Dry at first, than a small burn as it went down. Hmm. Not bad.

Jordan took another swallow. Sammy jumped up onto the couch and curled up to Jordan. He absently scratched the cat's ear.

"Dipping into that pretty heavy, aren't ya?" Jim asked.

"Yeah, so?"

One or two word answers were not the typical dialogue of his uncle. "Aunt Kayla will need you sober when she comes home."

"She doesn't need me." But Jordan did sit up and put his glass on the end table next to him.

Jim laughed. "You're so stupid."

Jordan's eyebrow lifted, but he said nothing.

"You two need each other so much it's disgusting sometimes." Jim set his glass down. "She didn't do this to hurt you. She did this to heal herself. Stop taking it so personally."

"I don't know what's worse. Living with a twenty-year-old who knows everything. Or living with a twenty-year-old who knows everything *and* is an amateur psychologist."

"It's a gift."

They both laughed, but it ceased. A car approached.

"Uncle Jordan?"

A car door opened, slammed shut.

"Hmm?"

Another door.

"Stop being so stupid now, okay?"

Jordan rose and took a deep breath. "Okay."

Chapter Twenty

"I wish you would tell me what happened," begged Maggie.

Turning her gaze from the whizzing cars on interstate 81 back towards Maggie, Kayla sighed. They were about twenty minutes from Duncan and had spoken very little since she came out of the doctor's office. Stunned by how her life had totally changed in the hour she'd spent with Dr. Holling, Kayla now had difficulty unscrambling her jumbled thoughts. "It's all kind of mixed up in my head right now. I need to think it through, absorb it."

"At least tell me if you're going to be all right."

"I swear. I'm fine. Just no questions right now, okay?"

Reluctantly, Maggie relinquished her inquiry. "Okay."

Arriving at Kayla's house, Jordan appeared in the doorway. He held the door open as Kayla went into the house, with Maggie right behind her. Kayla wheeled to the living room. She saw Jim by the couch, a wine glass next to him.

"Are you feeling okay?" she asked.

"Yes," Jim replied. "Are you?"

She understood and appreciated his concern. "Yeah, I think so." It was still jumbled, but the edges were beginning to smooth out.

"I think I'll go to bed early. We'll talk tomorrow, Aunt Kayla?"

She smiled. "You bet."

Kayla watched Jim leave after he set the wineglass on the end table.

She continued forward until she was in front of the living room window. Maggie exchanged words with Jordan, but Kayla continued to look out the window. Slowly meshing together her thoughts, her mind absorbed, acclimated, and finally accepted the outcome of her visit to Dr. Holling. Her gaze roamed the sky that was beyond the panes of the window. When the last thought clicked into place, she spotted a shooting star. She grinned.

"Kay, I think I'll be going home now."

Kayla turned to see Maggie walk up beside her. "Thanks for everything." She saw the concern in Maggie's eyes, so she added, "I'll be okay. Honest."

Maggie bent and gave her a teddy bear hug. "Call me if you need anything."

"I will."

Maggie turned, gave Jordan a quick hug, and left.

Kayla turned her attention to Jordan. His gaze roamed over her and his body was stiff, rigid. "Would you like something to drink, something to eat?" he asked.

"No, Jordan. I'm fine."

He hesitantly walked to her. Bending down, he took her hands, and quietly pleaded, "Tell me. Tell me what happened."

"I'm not going through with the procedure." Amazing how easy it was to say it now. The words tripped slightly over the residual hurt but they all stumbled out together. This was final. Dancing was never going to be a possibility again. "I was mad at first. Hurt. Disappointed."

Jordan squeezed her hands then brushed a tear from her cheek. She hadn't realized she'd been crying.

"Oh, Kay, I'm sorry. I didn't realize, really *realize*, how badly you wanted this. How much you needed to know. I guess I've been selfish, not wanting you to have the procedure. I was just so afraid that you thought you *needed* to change. And I was afraid that if you did change, you wouldn't need me anymore."

"Oh, Jordan, that's stupid."

"I've been told that already."

"It's done now," she said with a degree of acceptance. "But there is—"

The shrill ring of the phone interrupted her.

"Damn! I've been expecting a call from the nursery," Jordan said. "This'll just take a minute."

He got up, brushed a quick kiss on her brow. Kayla

watched Jordan's retreating back. The news she'd bottled up inside threatened to boil over. Holding it in all day had made her anxious, excited, scared. Busting at the seams, she felt the need to say it. Now.

As Jordan turned the corner, Kayla blurted, "I'm pregnant."

Only a second later, Jordan returned to the doorway he'd just vacated. "Excuse me?"

The phone still rang, but Kayla thought she had Jordan's undivided attention now. She couldn't help but giggle. The look on his face resembled a deer caught in a car's headlights. There was silence when the phone ceased ringing and Jordan, again, kneeled down in front of her.

"That's why I can't go through with the procedure," she continued. "I'm pregnant."

"But—"

"I was sad. Angry. Disappointed. But then Dr. Holling told me I was pregnant. He admitted I could try the procedure, but it hadn't been tried on pregnant women. So he couldn't say for sure what would happen." Kayla laughed at Jordan's bemused expression. "That must've been what I looked like when he told me." She paused, and spoke softly some of the most sacred and beautiful words she'd ever said. "We're going to have a baby."

This time her news got through to him. Jordan leapt at her and hugged her tightly. In a whisper, he asked, "A baby?" He pulled away and gazed into her eyes.

"He did the test twice to be sure." Feeling ecstatic, Kayla couldn't hold her laughter in. She knew she must have sounded like a giddy drunk. But her laughter ceased when she saw the seriousness on his face. "What?"

"What about the procedure? What about—"

"It's taken me awhile," she interrupted, "to get it, to understand where I was coming from. From the second I woke up in that hospital room twenty years ago, I believed I had to change myself to get what I wanted. When we met, you showed me I didn't have to change to find happiness. But old dreams, old insecurities, came to the surface when I saw that magazine article. Once again I had this need to *fix* me, to make me *right*. But when Dr. Holling told me I was pregnant, I felt right. Whole."

Jordan still looked puzzled, so she elaborated. "A week ago, Maggie made a point I didn't fully understand 'til today. I'm happy, Jordan. I've got everything I've ever dreamed of: a home, a fulfilling job, you, Jim, and now this baby. And I haven't had to change to get all of that. I haven't had to be in a perfect body, in a perfect world to get what I wanted. I just had to be me. When Dr. Holling discussed the uncertainty of doing the procedure on me now that I'm pregnant, I was faced with a choice: my past or my future. Knowing that this life grew inside of me, I choose my future."

Slowly, his lips curved into a smile. When his smile bloomed to a giant grin, he said, "Not only do I love you, but I *like* you too."

Kayla smiled in return. Everything seemed possible now. Everything felt right now. After twenty years of self-hate and self-doubt, of disappointment and grief, of self-growth and acceptance, she was finally proud of whom she was and she understood why she was here. Through unimagined pain and the healing power of love, she'd finally become comfortable with being Kayla Jennings Michaels. She grasped this feeling of unabashed contentment and tucked it away in her heart.

It wouldn't be perfect, she mused. Carrying and delivering her child could be risky. Traveling the twists and turns of motherhood would be tricky. Hoping and praying for her child's happiness and fulfillment would be constant. But the very fact that she faced these novel subjects meant that it was a reality. Despite all the negatives of the past, including hostile peers, Rob, and her own self-doubt, Kayla had not only beaten the odds, she'd surpassed them. She would beat them again, she knew. And this time she would have Jordan along with her on the journey.

He placed his hand on her lower abdomen. "Here?"

Tears of unimagined happiness sprung to Kayla's eyes. "Yes."

He tenderly rubbed her belly, sending warmth skipping up into her heart. "Hey, you, I'm your dad. I can't wait to see you."

In that moment, Kayla knew complete and utter joy. Her happiness was ironic, really. In that one instant, a dream died. But it died a quick, soundless death and was immediately replaced. A new vibrant dream was born, one that took hold and hugged her warmly, tightly. The life-sustaining warmth of that dream soothed her soul. She hadn't physically danced in twenty years. But as Kayla smiled down at Jordan's glowing face, she realized that her soul had found another way to dance. And this dance would last forever.

Later that night, Kayla and Jordan made slow, tender love to celebrate the good news. Afterwards, pleasantly exhausted, Kayla slipped into the night-time world where reality is reflected in a mirage of skewed images.

She was dancing in the sun-drenched fields, with various flowers brightening the meadow's landscape. As she danced, something on a lily made her stop and bend down to it. There, upon the flower's white petals, was a butterfly, its wings a brilliant blue. Enthralled by the insect, she watched as, slowly, its wings fluttered up and down as it inspected each waxen petal of the lily. After only a few moments, the butterfly flew away.

And she began to dance again.